MERCY'S QUEST:

THE RETURN

BY
EAST S.M.

ISBN:979-8-9852589-1-2

Library of Congress Control Number: 2022937875

Any references to historical events, real people, or real places are used fictitiously. Names, characters, and places are products of the author's imagination.

Front cover image and illustrations by Fabio Listrani
Book design by Jessica Stooksbury

First printing edition 2022
Published by Auguries and Alchemy
Knoxville, TN

auguriesandalchemy.com

*For my love who comforts my
heart and encourages me.*

*For my family who
empowers me.*

*For Venus whose brightness
holds my darkness.*

TABLE OF CONTENTS

Chapter 1

Appalachian Mountain Witch

Autumn evenings deserve the enchantment of fire. The smell of smoke drifting to the stars, the glow of flames dancing as lovers, the sound of the heat as it crackles and grows. But this fire is different. Tonight, I am not enchanted. Tonight, the world is burning.

Before me, the eyes of everyone I know stare, unblinking, and in them I see the chains of the heaviest sorrow I have ever witnessed. They stand waiting, warming by the fire as the cool wind blows through my body. My consciousness teeters in and out. My mind is confused; the darkness without and within envelops me, confining the light that made me. Nevertheless, my body knows, knows what is happening. Suddenly, time catches up with itself, and I am fully present. I swiftly look left and right, horrified, and as I reluctantly look down, the scene declares its truth in an instant. My shallow breath searches for its last ounce of strength.

I will myself in this moment to accept the fate around my neck. Lord Death has this uncomplicated elegance in meeting you where you are in such a state. It is like a dance between intimate partners. Light rushes through my spirit, an elixir of grace pouring into my body, and I take in my final scene one more time, hanging from the very tree where I prayed for their wellbeing.

I must be loved to draw such a sorrowful tribe of souls. The scene before me begins its soft fade.

Grace is now consuming my light. My toes are warming, my body ready. As the caw of a crow explodes through the sky, I lock eyes with my executioner. With ferocious force, lightning strikes the ground. In this very moment, with the confidence of 10,000 warhorses, I take my last breath.

Thunder crashed, quaking the ground and waking me from the nightmare I could not seem to escape. That must have been the thirteenth night in a row. As I gratefully returned to my physical body, gripping the sheets and snuggling my pillow just to prove to myself that this was reality, I heard my Mim humming softly in the kitchen.

The smell of biscuits and gravy lightened the heaviness in my chest from another restless night. Of all the many gifts my grandmother possessed, cooking was her most magnificent. She prepared food with perfect mindfulness, approaching it like a painter constructing a masterpiece. She believed the energy of your being should be aware of the healing you deliver through nourishing others. Food has an opportunity to comfort and ground people when they need love the most. There is nothing in the world like the experience that is Mim's kitchen, and I felt so glad I was about to shake away that horrible nightmare and center myself with some of her Appalachian soul food.

Agnes Faye Stone was known as Aggie to her friends, Mim to her grandchildren, and the ol' witch of Moon Ruth Hollow to the townspeople. She was the one who gave me my nickname Mercy, short for Emerson. Her intention behind this choice, she told me, was that I always hold compassion and forgiveness above all things. She would say, "Child, you are more powerful than you know. Your bloodline is the most respected of all among the witch folk who walk this earth. It is crucial to those around you that you learn the true meaning of servitude. We are here to help and guide." I responded the way you might imagine an eight-year-old would; nevertheless, the nickname stuck.

"Mercy, is that you stirring 'round? Are you awake?"

"I'm awake," I mumbled. "Besides, how can anyone sleep with the aroma of your gifts flooding this house?"

I shuffled into the kitchen wearing my weariness on the surface, slowly making my way to the table. The smell of fresh bread, apples and cinnamon, and sage-kissed sausage filled the air. They smelled like safety and comfort. Food made with sacred, deep love and the direct spiritual intention of spell casting always sends empowerment and contentment through one's soul.

"You had one of your visions again, didn't you?" she said in that all-knowing, all-seeing tone.

"It was just a dream, Mim." The words came out through an uncertain yawn. I knew in my heart that it was not just a dream. As certain as I was that she was speaking volumes of truth, I was equally in a space of denial, not ready to face whatever was happening to me. The dreams were always the same. Some of them were very straightforward, some so peculiar I could barely wrap my mind around them.

Mim placed a plate of food under my sleepy face. The very first bite sent a surge of love through every level of my being. Homemade bread from a cast-iron skillet with sausage gravy was surely the cure-all for burdened minds all throughout these mountains. That skillet had been in our family for at least two generations. Mim always said iron signifies truth. She believed cooking from it adds a nudge towards self-discovery in every dish.

She also used a special stirring spoon, charming, with moons carved in the handle. Its reddish wood stain was still rich in color like a fresh, plump cherry.

She'd bought it years ago from a vendor selling wares at the Boone Annual Fall Festival. This artist told her the wood symbolized growth and life and that he had acquired the wood from an ancient tree. Aggie loved that spoon. Since that day, it had been her wand, stirring her cauldron of delicious magic.

With the sweetest smile, she placed her hand on my head, pulling my messy, long charcoal hair from my pale face. "Mercy, you can't run from destiny. Blood Moon witches have an agreement with this world. We are —"

"The living embodiment of the Death card. I know, Mim."

"You make light, child, but that includes you! We are here to help facilitate the evolution of humanity. You'll see, Mercy. The people who need your knowing will find you."

I sat silently, lost in thought, as Mim went to the stove to clean up the aftermath of her morning love offering.

Mim did everything gracefully. Floating like a feather carried by a gentle autumn breeze, she walked with an aura of strength and stealth. My aura was quite the opposite, I was well aware. I felt my heart pump, announcing its deep yearning, heavy and focused on my upcoming travels to see Auntie Maxine.

Madame Maxine Flora Jones was my grandmother's younger sister. Great Auntie Max was a priestess for the Temple of the Moons. She was the Matriarch of our magic, the grandest Blood Moon Mage of our time. She was known for drawing down the sacred energy from all the moons in the Universe and channeling it into her spiritual work to help the people of her city, the Crescent City of hidden magic—New Orleans.

"You thinking 'bout Max?"

Mim always felt her sister when my thoughts drew her essence into a room. I nodded confirmation of her unerring intuition.

"She is ready for you, Emerson Stone. I can feel it. The dreams. Your growing internal hunger for something missing. The deepening of this relationship with your handsome lesson."

Suddenly the blood rushed from my pounding heart to my head. "Abel isn't a lesson, Mim! He is my calm, my tether. He keeps me grounded."

She laughed. "As if being grounded is truly what you want right now. Sweet love, the howl of the sacred winds is calling you to a journey. It is all over you. I know it, and you know it. It is time for your ascension."

We stared at each other, two strong women with an extra connection to the rhythms of this world. We loved each other fiercely, but we both knew that the path of the women in our bloodline was a path of solitude, a navigation through the sacred, full of adventure but also aloneness.

Mim hugged me close. "Enjoy your last day at work, Mercy. I know it's only a few months, but I'm sure gonna miss you while you're helping Max."

I flashed the warmest smile at my grandmother. Her love made me feel like I was immortal, strong enough to handle anything. I could not say it back to her, but I would miss her just as much.

I quickly got ready for my day, jumped in my old '77 Ford truck, and off to the Mooney Holler Cafe I went. My family had owned the little store for almost a hundred years. We kept a modest variety of canned goods and other staples, plus a produce section from our family garden, along with other items of need for folks in the surrounding hollows. Adjacent to the produce section was a makeshift kitchen laboratory. My mother, Diana, was an herbalist whose concoctions were available to those brave enough to try the nontraditional approach to healing. She had something for almost any disease of the mind, body, and spirit. Her brother, my Uncle Ezra, ran the coffee-and-sweets shop in the front. Throughout the store were paintings created by my father, Thomas Ayers. He spent all his time in his studio painting landscapes from realms far beyond this earth. I offered intuitive bodywork through massage and energy healing. Quite controversial for this little conservative mountain town, but also quite successful because everyone has a side of shadow within them. People around here loved to judge our family like we were their Devil, but secretly they ran to us when they needed our help.

Our family had always been shadow healers. When the light inside someone is blocked, a shadow is created. Into the shadow, we cast our magic. With our powers, we could shift the energies inside people to help them return to wholeness. With each individual we restored, our family helped maintain the balance of light and dark on this planet. This is the tradition I was born into, and I could feel my powers growing within me every day. As much as I feigned dismissiveness in front of Mim, I knew that I could not avoid the messages of my dreams any longer. I needed answers. I was ready to know more about who I was becoming.

That's why I was going to see Auntie Max. I'd never met anyone else like us until the age of seven, when I first went to visit her in New Orleans. To this day, my family members are the only witches who have ever lived in the little old town of Boone, Kentucky.

Boone was birthed by brothels and saloons and the dreams of struggling Englishmen in the late 1800s. Even now, the town is saturated with an energy both hopeful and desperate. The Stones came over with a handful of other families from England because the town was promised to be an "enchanted place." My great-great-grandmother Aramintha, in all her intuitive wisdom, knew this was where she needed to settle her family. The Stones became the first, and only, witches to settle in Boone, Kentucky, bringing their blood moon magic to Appalachia. Moon Ruth Hollow, known as Mooney Holler to locals, is where almost all my family live. At the fork at the entrance to the hollow, you can choose to go either right or left, depending on the nature of your visit. The left fork is for those seeking a sense of the sacred and calm. The right is full of wild mystery: weed dealers, mysterious Appalachian creatures, and strange lights all throughout those woods. We had family scattered throughout both sides, and our cafe was at the entrance where the forks meet by the main road.

My Uncle Ezra met me in the parking lot as I was pulling into the cafe. "I heard you storming through the Holler long before you made it here. Mercy, you need to get that exhaust fixed. Go on now, Ms. Edna is waiting on you in the back."

I jumped out of my truck, hugged him, and went to my office.

"Good morning, Ms. Edna!"

"Mercy, I tell you, I wouldn't be able to move if it wasn't for our weekly sessions."

Such a kind soul. I hugged her gently. "We will get started as soon as I set the space."

"Take your time, child. At this age, I'm in a hurry for nothing at all."

Edna was a resident of Boone from the other side of town. A sassy seventy-nine-year-old, she used to be the town psychic and tarot reader. These days, her divination consisted mostly of studying the Farmers' Almanac to find the best time to tend to her garden. Edna was Mim's best friend and the only other nontraditional soul around these parts. The two became very close after my Auntie Maxine moved away. I saw her for bodywork every Saturday at 9:30 a.m.

The closing of the curtains encouraged the room to surrender to darkness. The delicate smoke of Palo Santo lent its sweetness to cleanse the area. As Ms. Edna relaxed into the moment, I placed a large jade stone under the table, an act of prayer and respect from my heart to hers. While working on her, I found myself losing ground. My thoughts drifted to my dream from the night before. I took a breath and focused on the sound of rushing water. Easily I fell back into the rhythm of the work.

I finished the massage and whispered, "Ms. Edna, I'll meet you up front when you're ready. Take your time."

We always sat down for tea and my Uncle Ezra's famous peanut butter fudge after every session. I picked the table by the window facing the Holler. Edna walked out of the room with the stride of a twenty-year-old. She understood the value of total bodywork.

"Thank you. My mobility and energy have been restored. I felt you drift and then reground. What has you troubled, dear? Would you like a reading?"

Before I could answer, she pulled out her deck and handed them to me to shuffle.

"Edna, I don't know what's happening. I am restless. I keep having these crazy dreams about -"

"Visions," she interrupted.

"Visions. About death, the moon, space." My words were hushed by the sound of rain on the tin roof of the cafe. Uncle Ezra loved to keep the doors open when the temperature was exactly right, and a late summer storm was on the rise. The sound of nature's natural expression filled the cafe.

Edna pulled a sewing needle from her purse, prompting a sweet memory from long ago. Mim taught me this special method when I was a girl. Blood holds the essence of our deepest truth, and this kind of magic required an offering. Edna lit the candle on the table. I offered her my index finger.

"Ouch!"

"You still haven't gotten used to this, have you, child?" She laughed, squeezing a tiny drop of blood into the flame.

"Let me have the deck, and let's see what Spirit wants you to see." She stacked the deck between us on the table and closed her eyes, with her left hand creating an umbrella over the deck.

I loved watching Ms. Edna in the throes of divination. Something about the space she held shifted any mundanity within her to timeless sacred knowing. She hovered in a prayerful state for what felt like forever and then cut the cards swiftly into three stacks — past, present, and future. Then she flipped the top card of each, revealing the Six of Cups, the Lovers, and, finally, for the future, the Chariot. I knew tarot, and normally I would understand what this reading meant, but there was an image in my mind distracting me from the wisdom on the table. Edna, incredibly tuned in as always, grabbed my hand and said, "What are you feeling, Mercy?"

"I feel cold," I replied. "In my mind's eye, I see a gray cloak." As I spoke this vision, thunder roared in the distance, and the rain fell heavily, foretelling the magnitude of the incoming storm.

"Emerson Buckley Stone, you have quite the adventure ahead of you. A tale of travel and a relationship that will shift focus to your past."

"I see Abel only sporadically. Working with Maxine for a few months will hopefully provide an opportunity for us to have more time together. Maybe this restlessness is about us deepening our connection to each other, letting go of the past and creating a future together." No sooner had I spoken the words when suddenly all became quiet. No rain. No traffic. No cicadas singing in the trees.

"If I were you, dear, I would not attach meaning to this reading just yet. I have a feeling this reading is reaching far beyond your current connections. Be open to a past beyond your knowing and a future beyond your expectations." A crow squawked, and instantly, like a faucet turning on, the rain started pouring again.

I sipped my tea and watched from the big window as crows mined worms in the grass. That squawk struck a familiar chord in my heart. I sat in peaceful silence with Edna eating my treat and contemplating the reading. As I gazed in the distance toward the highest branch on a tree across from us, I saw something moving.

"Well, I've got chickens to check in on," Edna said, interrupting my reverie. "This storm will get worse before it gets better, much like your path." She winked at me while downing the last sip of jasmine tea. Cryptic statements were commonly delivered in my circle of people. We lived in a land of mysterious messages laced with warning and hope. Upon standing, Ms. Edna noticed a card had floated from her deck underneath the table. It was the Three of Swords. As I handed it over to her, she said, "Oh, there is an opportunity for growth ahead of you, child."

I walked Ms. Edna to her car and heard the crow squawk again. It was coming from the treetop that had caught my gaze just minutes before. I looked up to find the initiator of this familiar call flying towards me. It landed three feet in front of me.

"A white crow!" I shouted. "In all my life, I have never seen such a thing. How beautiful … ." My words were broken by Ms. Edna's hand harshly grabbing and firmly pulling my left arm.

"Mercy, stop walking."

But I couldn't stop. I was moving in a trance toward this mysterious crow. Every step I took, she took a step back, as if she were leading me into the woods. I had somehow walked about five feet forward, with Ms. Edna cautiously following, until she felt the need to break our connection. I stared into the crow's eyes and she into mine. We knew each other. I don't know how I knew, but the knowing consumed me. Together the crow and I were floating on a sea of otherworldly awareness, familiarity, and bliss. She squawked again, and …

Edna yelled frantically, "Mercy! Mercy, are you OK? Ezra, we need you outside!"

The world came back into focus as a misting rain blanketed me. Uncle Ezra picked me up off the ground.

"Took a little tumble, did you, Mercy?" He brushed the dirt off my knee as one would a child.

"She passed out, Ezra." Edna turned to me and took both my hands into hers. "Mercy, white crows are messengers of the unknown. Shadow birds. You were enchanted by this one. Stay out of the woods until you leave Appalachia. These mountains have secrets in their depths that even Aggie cannot wrap her mind around. It's best that you take it easy today."

Uncle Ezra stepped in. "Diana can handle the rest of the day without you. Take the afternoon to rest, and we'll see you at your farewell dinner tonight."

I was so shaken that I didn't argue. I grabbed my things from inside the cafe and jumped back into my truck. Turning down the right fork of the Holler, headed toward home, I had the urge to be in the mountain. Nature was my safe space, and I really needed to process what just happened. I passed my house and continued driving. There were a couple of old mining roads that branched off up to the mountain at the end of the fork. My favorite one led to a cave at the top of the peak.

I parked my truck, grabbed my lantern, and walked on the small path to the cave. Appalachian caves are the sources of all kinds of cautionary tales. According to the older generation, Appalachian Fey Folk, Bigfoot creatures, bobcats and bears wandered the caves and abandoned mining shafts. I grew up hanging out in this cave, and although I felt comfort in this familiar space, I never went past a certain point in the darkness.

A hundred feet from the entrance was an underground stream. Maybe it was the rushing water, or maybe it was being further in the mountain, but whatever the reason, the temperature dropped dramatically at that point. The frigid air reinforced what my instinct was screaming. I knew I was not welcome to go any farther. I guess that energy was what always drew me in. This cave had become my sanctuary. Staring toward the unexplored path, I was reminded that I belong to the Unknown.

There was a large flat rock that protruded over the running water with a smooth surface, perfect for sitting. When I was nine years old, I named that rock Saturn's Bridge. The irony of daydreaming about space in my cavernous lair seemed as relevant today at twenty-six as it did when I was a child. That rock had the power to recharge me. I sat there thinking about all the dreams. Abel. The reading with Edna. That white crow. If only divination could give concrete answers. Choices should be considered more cautiously when divine guidance has been cast. I knew I was facing something enormous.

I took a deep breath and pulled peace into my belly. The cave stream always had this way of connecting me to Source. Its water spoke to me the essence of the unknown and transformation from the womb of the earth. As my heart found my inner quiet, I took a deep cleansing breath, thanked my environment, and made my exit from the sanctuary. When I arrived at the cave's entrance, the rain had picked back up. I made my way down to my truck and headed home, soaking wet.

Mim was busy preparing the house for guests to arrive for my sendoff dinner. In her mind, being gone longer than two weeks warranted celebratory feasts. I needed to get out of my wet clothes. I drew a bath with fresh lavender, eucalyptus, and rose petals and let the aromas nurture my heart with sweetness and receptivity.

I heard an unfamiliar voice in our foyer. Aggie was in full-service mode. I could tell because her voice was raised an octave. It was surely a townie needing supernatural guidance. The townies loved the dramatic aspects of witchery, the show. They were drawn to our powers, but they were always afraid that if they met the true face of magic it would be too much for them to handle. So we comically articulated our words to accommodate their fairytale; hence, Mim welcoming in this person with her Glenda the Good Witch voice. I heard Mim setting out the teapot and knew she must be doing a reading. I walked into the family room to find a stranger examining a family heirloom, an antique box Mim kept on the mantle. He was a very handsome gentleman, dressed extremely well. Definitely not a townie. He wore brown pants with soft tan stripes and a burgundy shirt that screamed Old World fashion. As magnificent as his presence was his scent, a blend of sweet tobacco and saffron with a hint of raw ginger. Taking in his fragrance, I became lost in a lingering afternote of vetiver. It intoxicated my senses, taking me back to my cave. No one could resist a scent like that.

I became suddenly aware that I was very close to this strange man, involuntarily drawn to him by his scent. I pretended I had intended to get up in his personal space by offering a handshake. "Hello, my name is Emerson. And you are …?"

"Ash Sullivan. Pleased to make your acquaintance."

He had an accent I couldn't place. He took my hand and kissed the back of it in the gentlest fashion. Definitely not from around here.

"This box is quite fascinating," he said, returning his attention to the object of his interest. "The detail is magnificent."

Aggie walked in with her cups and special blend of loose-leaf tea.

"Mercy, this is Mr. Sullivan. He is a guest lecturer at the university and researching Appalachian divination while in town. Uncle Ezra referred him our way when he stopped by the cafe." Mim made her way back to the kitchen to check on her teapot.

"Mercy? That's an interesting name," he said, chuckling. "Mercy, could I be so bold as to ask you to tell me about this box? There's something quite compelling about it."

I didn't like how he made the statement regarding my name as if it were some irony to which I was oblivious, but I indulged him anyway. The truth was, there was something quite compelling about him, too. Before I could answer, though, Agatha Faye, with her divine timing, floated into the room with a teapot in one hand and a tarot deck in the other. "That old box has been in our family for years." She fixed Ash with a commanding gaze. "Please, sit."

Mim had him sip the tea, all the while engaging him in conversation. Ash was deeply knowledgeable about many esoteric topics, so you best believe Agatha Faye Stone was hanging on every word that came from his lips. As her granddaughter, I knew exactly what Mim was up to. She believed offering people homemade treats and kind conversation made their energy more authentic, which led to a more holistic reading than one focused on a specific question. Oftentimes, people get in their own way energetically, which can muddy how they receive messages from Spirit. Mim felt showing up at the tea table was enough for the Universe to see your needs. Several layers of wisdom can come from one single cup. In addition to the tea leaves, she would pull a single card at the end to outline the immediate future of the person. The time came to swirl the last sip, and when he finished, Mr.

Sullivan cautiously placed the cup upside down on the saucer. Mim picked up the cup and began her reading.

"I see mountains and isolation. A chain promises that a significant series of events is about to take place. The chain is placed strategically by a rune, a symbol for courage while facing destiny. Fate is heavy in this reading. A woman is linked to your fate. She will travel east to find you. The top of the cup represents your future. A pyramid with a moon inside. To the right of the pyramid, a star with wings. I am not one to force an intuitive thought during a reading, so I will admit, I am unfamiliar with these symbols and can only deduce that it's speaking of a message — wings—coming from a space of illumination — star — and the pyramid is an actual person, place, or thing." Aggie stared at the cup, deep in concentration.

"You seem lost in thought, Ms. Stone," Ash said, seemingly unaffected by the reading.

"In sixty years of readings, you, sir, are an impenetrable wall. My readings are a combination of energy assessment and tea-leaf guidance, but I could rely only on the symbols for you. Your energy is removed from my sight. Let us see what card is sitting with your future." Mim turned over the top card, and the Devil was staring back at her.

Ash, with a devious grin, remarked, "Well, nothing says you're living fully like the Devil in your future. Thank you very much, Ms. Stone. I have taken up enough of your time. It was a pleasure meeting you." He handed a hundred-dollar bill to my grandmother. Ash stared intentionally at the box before casting a hard gaze at me. "Emerson, until we meet again." Swiftly he made his way to his car and left our home.

Until we meet again? He sounded strangely confident.

"What a strange fellow, Mim," I said.

"I found him quite fascinating." Her voice was excited, reflecting on what had transpired.

"I wonder why he was so mesmerized with that box."

"It's an enchanted totem. Of course Mr. Sullivan was drawn to it. He's an occultist."

I picked up the box and carefully examined its markings like I had done a thousand times before. It was solid black. A Roman numeral, X, was etched in gold in the center. Two crescent moons, one on each side, were almost like the triple goddess symbol. The bottom of the box had an inscription: "Scattered in preservation. When lost, look for roots in the sky, not the ground." The box had an unusual lock on the side with three letters etched into the lock: L.A.S. The key was lost generations ago, so we don't know what's inside. Oddly, no one had made the attempt to solve that mystery, as it seemed like an unspoken reverence not to. A boundary was placed there for a reason.

The mist looked spooky as it lay heavy in a post-storm sunset. One by one, my family members came in to wish me safe travels. Edna brought her famous apple pie. Other neighbors popped in and out. They knew when Agatha Stone cooked, there was plenty for everyone. Staple dishes of the mountain decorated the table: cornbread, greens, fresh garden vegetables, fried chicken, and beans. The feast would be available throughout the evening, with coffee, pie, and conversation closing the night out. We sat on the porch listening to the sounds of nature at dusk. My favorite was the rainwater cascading like a miniature waterfall over the side of the mountain. Ezra and Edna filled Mim in on the details of the white crow incident earlier that day. Our interesting customer Ash Sullivan got a brief mention. My grandmother described him enthusiastically to all who would listen. I didn't blame her excitement. We don't usually get to be so open with customers about our ways. As Mim spoke, I could feel Ash's presence, solid and heavy. Maybe I was making something out of nothing, but I sensed a deep connection to him.

Between him, Edna's reading, and the white crow, I didn't know what to think. I learned growing up in a magical world that it's best to surrender to the chaos and learn to work within the weird and unexpected. Fear and resistance to the pull of destiny only creates a longer road and unnecessary pain. I decided I would remain as open as I could to the growing strangeness around and changes within.

The guests left a few at a time, and when everyone had gone, I lay in bed thinking about what was ahead of me. A text message from Abel asking my ETA made my heart pound with anticipation. I loved my mountain, but I could not wait to dip my soul into the Big Easy. With my thoughts consumed by Abel, I fell into a deep sleep.

Fog lays over the river like a swaddled baby. I find myself wandering again in a familiar yet unknown land. This is not the sky I know; instead, it's creamy orange with a red moon above and stars scattered throughout. I am hovering above water, floating slowly toward a bank. Directly in front of me lies a stone pathway illuminated in green aventurine. My face is covered in some sort of strange fabric, yet my vision is perfectly clear. I am wearing a long gray cloak. My breath draws rolling icy vapors with every cast, yet my body feels no temperature. Neutral comfort and a sense of weightlessness surround my being, yet, ironically, my feet are very grounded. My body is a source of light that is being pulled to its desired location. There is a sound coming from the distance.

"Caw-Caw".

I woke up frantically, startled, half-realizing I was having one of three recur-
ring dreams.

"Caw-Caw".

Wait. That wasn't my dream. That was coming from outside. I peeked over
the blanket, looking out of my bedroom window, and there she was: the white
crow. She was perched on the hood of my truck in the driveway, staring directly
at me through my bedroom window. I hopped out of bed and ran outside,
only to discover she had flown away. A key with a familiar design was placed
in the center of my truck's hood. I ran inside with haste, and Mim already
was holding the box as if she knew this was coming.

"I had a vision, Mercy. A lady dressed in a gray cloak walking on the edge of a
lake came to me. Her face was covered, and she pointed her finger at me. As
the ruby ring she wore illuminated, bright as the moon, she said, 'The time
has come.' I was awakened to the sound of this box crashing on the floor."

As Mim was carefully putting the box back in its place on the mantle, I
whispered, "I have the key, Mim."

She turned around and asked, "You have the key? How?"

"My destiny is unfolding, and the timing of the trip affirms things are about
to get very interesting for me."

With conviction, I walked to the box, and without hesitation, I opened it. What was revealed would forever change the direction of my life as I knew it — a perfectly preserved human finger adorned with a ruby ring.

CHAPTER 2

Down in New Orleans

I moved in with my grandmother about three years ago when she started having health concerns after a minor heart scare. Leaving her now after recent revelations weighed on my own heart as I loaded my last bag of belongings into my truck. The summer woods were alive with the sounds of the hollow. Cicadas buzzing in unison deep in the thick woods serenaded us all with a hypnotizing cadence to welcome the day. Uncle Ezra's roosters were also doing their morning job of announcing the day's first light. But then Agatha Faye Stone, queen of this mountain, stepped out of the doorway, and it drew them to a reverent pause. Her mere presence was a reminder of the role we play as effectors on this earth. She walked to meet me and hugged the breath right out of me.

"Mercy, I think it's best we keep this discovery to ourselves. Totems don't remain hidden from the world for so long just to be exposed by our ego's curious wonder. The story will continue to unfold; it always does. Your job is to stay in a space of active receptivity."

I knew she was right, but there was a twinge of doubt in my mind when I answered, "I will, Mim."

"I mean it, Mercy. It is no small thing that you have been gifted with this ruby, the original healing stone and the most powerful stone on Earth."

I often used stones in my bodywork, so I knew Mim was referring to the fact that rubies are the most coveted stones among healers, because of their ability to influence blood flow in the body. The ruby is prized for breaking down barriers to fertility, clearing blood clots and regulating pressures, making it the ultimate healing stone because of its impact on the human heart and its functions. It also intensifies emotions, which is essential to healing when the physical body is weak. If the mind sets itself to heal, a ruby will elevate that intention. This intensity must be handled with extreme skill and care. The ruby is a true ancient Old World blood stone.

I knew all this, but somehow I felt it wasn't the whole story, not when it came to this particular ruby. As if reading my mind, Mim gave me a knowing look and added, "There is talk of certain magical texts stating that all of the original stones come from other worlds unknown to the human inhabitants of Earth."

She held my hand as we walked to the truck and looked deep into my eyes, saying, "I will not encourage grounding, for I feel the wind needs your feet light for movement. Your mind needs to be open in ways it's never desired to be. I will not inspire a need for balance, as that peaceful stillness is not what currently promotes your growth. My wish for you is that you remain focused. Feed your body with foods that support your mission, lending you strength and clarity. May your grounding be found in your wisdom, not your feet. As the winds carry you through the unfolding of this great mystery, this becoming, may your magic illuminate like the moon, exerting power while commanding respect in the most magnificent ways from all who cross your path. Be careful, love. You came into this world with one foot already out of it. Trust divine order. You are a woman of action, always boldly walking towards your intended lessons wrapped in your ancestors' wisdom. That alone assures me that no harm will ever come to you."

She appeared visibly shaken but still spoke with such strength. I wrapped my arms around her, holding her as closely as I could. My grandmother was a powerful woman who seemed to have nothing on her mind but loving me. I promised her I would keep her posted on every single development.

"Mim, thank you for your wisdom and watchful eye. Nightmares and mysterious omens like the ones coming at me would instill fear in the heart, but you empower me to trust. I will take this step into my next chapter carrying the strength and honor of our fierce lineage. Take care of yourself. If the tea leaves speak from your cup any news of guidance, whisper them on the winds to me."

I gave her a kiss on the cheek and set off on my long drive to Louisiana. A sadness came over me as I pulled out of Moon Ruth Hollow onto the main road toward the highway. I knew the Emerson Buckley Stone that was leaving this hollow would never return. From my bones, I shuddered as a cold chill ran up my spine.

Ah, the freedom of the highway. Roads with a side of music created a holy space where I could be present to a world beyond my own knowing while examining the things that occupied my mind. Black Sabbath blaring through my speakers helped two hours of the eleven-hour trip fade away. Now that I'd settled into driving, I decided to call Abel. This man, this beautiful being, consumed me in every way. We communicated on a level outside of what we consciously knew. If our waking moments contained even a small dose of the true sacredness of our bond, then our bodies would choose to no longer exist in this world.

He answered in one ring. "Angel of Mercy, are you close?"

Just hearing the way his New Orleans accent spun his words, I visualized his perfect beauty: Eyes as dark as the damned and a soul so full of longing it took the breath out of me. His body was strong yet wore every emotion he'd ever felt. He was a warrior drenched in ambition but still touched by traces of vulnerability and feelings of rejection. I was in love with this man who was the living embodiment of tortured beauty. Yet we rarely saw one another. Dark mystery, a persistent theme woven through my story, the unknown ghost haunting me since birth.

"Not as close as I'd like to be. I should be crossing the bridge into the city around five p.m. Do you want to meet on Frenchmen for a drink around nine? Also, please stop calling me Angel of Mercy. It's weird." I laughed as that last sentence rolled dramatically off my tongue.

He laughed. "Nine it is. Safe travels, Mercy."

Hours passed with ease thanks to my shadowy musical playlist of doom metal. A pleasant montage of state signs passed by one after another in between sludgy guitar riffs that hypnotized me in the most satisfying way. Tennessee, Alabama, and finally Mississippi, passed. I had endured this long drive many times, and Hattiesburg, Mississippi was a marker letting me know I had only two more hours to go before arriving to the land under the sea, the Crescent City. In honor of traditions of the road, I always stopped there to get gas and stretch. As I filled up the tank, the Delta heat burned hot like the fire and mystery that consumed my soul. A familiar caw interrupted my road-weary, wandering thoughts, and in my search for the source of this squawk, I noticed a man who seemed to be having car trouble at the pump next to me. His car was full of canvases, musical instruments, and other interesting objects.

"Nice truck. Is it a '78?" he asked as he walked into my personal space to more closely examine my truck. His honey-colored hair, vintage Ozzy shirt, and blue eyes complemented the grease stains on his hands.

"Kentucky tags, too! What part of the Bluegrass State are you from?"

Oh, great, another desperate male who doesn't understand boundaries, I thought. Coldly, I responded, "Do you always make a habit of invading the space of a woman traveling alone? It's a '77, by the way." OK, so I couldn't help it; I had to engage. Something about him had drawn me in.

He extended his hand to shake mine: "H. Chambers Hoon."

As I placed my hand in his, a shock ran through both of our bodies that went beyond a basic static reaction. His car started by itself. We disconnected, and out of the corner of my eye, I saw a white crow slyly perched on a street sign across the road.

"I've been working on this car for twenty minutes, and suddenly you show up like an angel of the road, and my obstacle magically removes itself. What's your name, Kentucky?"

"Angels are for the lost, attached to a world I don't exist in," I retorted. "My name is Emerson." I kept one eye on him and the other on the crow, trying not to show any reaction to expose this magical creature whose mystery clearly was following me.

"Ms. Emerson from Kentucky, who's definitely not an angel," he said with a laugh, "thank you for lending your magic to my troubles. Safe travels, Kentucky." He threw a hand up as he pulled away from the pump. In the same moment, my mystery shadow flew up and disappeared into the sky. Lost in confusion, sweat dripping down my back, I was left to ponder yet another strange occurrence. I took this analysis to the road, returning to my mission of arriving safely in my new, temporary home.

Hoon was right. Magic did start that car: my magic. Something about our connection amplified what already existed inside of me. Yet he did not bat an eye to the reaction of our touch. Maybe he didn't feel what I felt. Maybe to him it was static electricity. Maybe it was a coincidence, and he really didn't know magic is alive and walking on this earth. H. Chambers Hoon. Who does that, anyway? I should consider a new introduction, E. Buckley Stone. I guess reducing your given name to an initial doubles your artistic cred these days. No matter, it had become clear that the white crow was watching me, and our family box with all its secrets was barely the beginning of a journey I felt would continue to unravel into the great unknown.

New Orleans delivers intensity the minute you penetrate her walls. Humidity soaked in veritas incantations, a thickening that permeates one's atmosphere, exposes one's hidden true substance. It is not a heaviness like a burden but rather a weight that comes from a deep wisdom woven into this earthly lowland by shadow magic unknown to the sages of this plane. The heat is a facilitator to this deep knowing. It leaves one with the choice of seeing only a meteorological inconvenience or submitting to her unspoken permission to operate from archaic primordial desires.

New Orleans wants you to go within, not look beyond. She is a seeker of inner truth for any foot that strokes her backbone. There is a similarity to the flow of life between the hidden hollows of Appalachia and this sea-level soul town. Small-town Appalachia and New Orleans share a slow pacing in the approach of their inhabitants, a vibe that allows no other choice but to accept its go-with-the-flow mentality. Existing in both places grooms an inner self-permission to take your time with your executions.

As I drove down Elysian Fields Avenue towards the Marigny district, the curious events from the past two days preoccupied my thoughts. I was primarily focused on the box. Whose finger was perfectly preserved in that box, and what was the white crow of mystery's connection with this totem? I would make it my mission here to research anything that would reveal the necessity of such an item. Surely a city saturated by the craft could provide me with some direction on how to find purpose in this exposed gift from the shadows.

My thoughts focused as I turned down the street I would call home for the next few months. Dauphine Street is full of New Orleans flavor. Shotgun houses are sprinkled one after another, each with a warm, tropical exterior. Auntie Maxine's house was no exception to the vibrancy, but it still stood out among the typical aesthetic of the block. She called her home 'the mountain below the sea.' This long, two-story home was painted forest green with black trimmed out edges and copper shutters with crescent moons etched in the frame. The porch was welcoming, with chunks of quartz and selenite placed strategically throughout. Rosemary adorned the property lines, a sentiment of wishes for peace among the living and the dead. I pulled my truck down the narrow alley to the back of the house where a small guest house was nestled nicely in the back corner of the small yard, a miniature version of the main house surrounded by large lavender bushes and yarrow. My new home away from home, I thought. I hopped out to find the whole neighborhood trying to catch a glimpse of me, when all of a sudden I was tackled in a hug.

"You sure know how to make an entrance with that loud beast you call transportation. The whole neighborhood is stirring. Let's get you settled quickly, and we'll meet Momma for dinner uptown." Louisa Mae Jones was tiny, but her voice carried even louder than my truck. Her long hair was dark as night, ringlets of curls creating a lovely exchange with the humidity as they brushed lightly around her waist. A smidge over five feet tall, with beauty that reached as high as the stars, LJ was Max's only daughter. She was born with the gift of comfort and charm and had this fierce ability to allow everyone around her to feel seen. She facilitated women's groups at the Temple of the Moons every Wednesday night, each one focusing on healing through movement. LJ was a stripper on Bourbon Street. She loved the freedom of sensual expression and felt it should not be suppressed by anyone who openly wanted to explore its gifts. I admired her fearlessness. In our family, freedom and power could be experienced in almost anything, even if it appeared on a nontraditional platform. I was happy to have her comfort during my stay.

There is an exchange, a sudden shift in energy, when the sun goes down in this town. The air comes alive with stealthy promises, and the heat has everyone dressed in as little clothing as possible. LJ and I walked into the restaurant, and in the corner sat my beautiful Auntie Max. Like Aggie, she had long, flowing hair, hers more silver than white. Her glasses, funky like her spirit, were cat-eye-shaped with an obnoxiously bold leopard print on the frame. Make no mistake, Madame Maxine Flora Jones was a woman of eccentricities on the inside as much as on the outside. She walked with a limp that forced her to keep a cane at her side. Her cane was topped by a falcon's head with eyes of iron.

"Evenin', Momma. You look fantastic, as always." LJ hugged Max and kissed her cheek. "I got Mercy all settled in. I think I'm going to sit at the bar and have a drink before we order food." She winked in her signature charming way. "Give you two a chance to catch up. Besides, the praline-covered bacon appetizer here is to die for, and I think I want it all to myself."

LJ proved her ability to quiet a room simply by walking to the bar. Her stride was executed from a subtle hip sway that delivered an illusion of gliding, like an apparition looking for trouble. She slithered, weaving in and out of the crowd, claiming her place at the center of the bar.

Maxine peered at me over the bridge of her glasses as she took a sip of coffee. "Mercy, you are looking weathered, my dear. How was the trip?"

"The trip was long," I answered, though I knew by "weathered" she meant more on the inside than on the surface.

"Mmmm. Three nights ago, I had the most intriguing dream." She slid her chair closer to mine, dropping her voice. "A figure walking in a cave wearing a gray robe extended a finger beyond her long, draping sleeve, pointing to the entrance. I followed the direction of her gesture to a pathway that opened to the side of a mountain. It was cold, so cold. Below the mountain stood a clan of people looking toward a grove of trees, although it was unclear to me what they were looking at. A gust of wind came from the cave, thrusting the gray cloak upward into the air, and suddenly the figure shifted into a gray crow. As she flew past me, the word 'Mercy' was whispered on the tail end of the wind. She flew toward the group, perching on a branch behind the clan of people. The branch held an entire murder. The sky abruptly exploded with thunder, and a white crow among the flock made the most tragic caw my ears have ever heard. I awoke. A sense of mourning crawled around my bones as I crept back to full awareness. Now I'll ask you plain, child. What did you bring to my doorstep? I can smell the secrecy on you."

Her intensity caused the lighting in the restaurant to flicker. All I could think of was Mim advising me to stay quiet for now.

"Things are unfolding in my life that I am not quite ready to articulate. My soul is holding certain details close. I am curious about your thoughts on animal guides, specifically, the white crow from your dream. I have encountered this feathered creature several times in the past few days, as recently as on the way here."

"White crow, you say?" She smiled, which was unnerving. A look of amusement was certainly not what I expected from her. "Animal guides provide us an opportunity to sit with that animal's specific gifts. In those moments lies an ability to see how applicable those qualities are to one's current circumstances." A sharp cackle escaped through her grin. "You know better than to ask such a generic question. Mercy, you are a Stone woman. You must speak to this creature and give yourself over to her wisdom. Animals reveal themselves to seekers like those in your precious Pythagorean Brotherhood through symbolism; however, our engagement with them is an entirely different matter. I can see we have a lot of work to do. You think you are here to help me with my overflow of clients seeking healing, but Aggie and I have secrets of our own."

Why was I not surprised?

"Your energy shifted when I mentioned Abel's family tradition. You must remember these devotees of soul searching wrapped in magical wonder may be appreciated in this world, but they are merely observers. Sure, they have an ability to channel magic. However, at the end of the day, they are human. What they barely tap into is the very source that we are created from. Our DNA has markings of magic, and theirs does not. Our essence is otherworldly and cannot be contained in a shell not fashioned by its origins." She tapped her cane on the floor one time like a gavel, a motion to emphasize her perspective on non-magically-born humans.

I felt the heat rise within me. This is not how I wanted to start my visit, but I found I must reply.

"I support the Brotherhood. They are passionate about the evolution of the soul in humanity. I feel their mission is the same as ours, to help and guide. Why are you and Mim so dismissive of them?"

"Now, now, Emerson, mind your emotions — and your elders."

The lights flickered again as her piercing gaze scanned my body. Suddenly, a calming sensation overrode the chill in my heart. Her intensity softened as she gently squeezed my hand. "It isn't that we are against them, or Abel. Most of the magic seekers on Earth have good aim regarding using the gifts of the unseen. They want to show people how to awaken their inner pathways to the collective motivated by their own self-discovery. But we would be foolish to turn a blind eye to their historically damning flaw: a need for power. Greed, wearing the suit of an obsession to know. They sense the great power in the gifted like us. Internal evolution, in part, is an acceptance that you are not meant to know all. A unique code programs every person's purpose, and knowledge is something that cannot be held by just anyone. It is as complex as it is simple. If I put all the magic in my body inside of a seeker, be it Pythagorean, hedge witch, healer, waiter, or banker, the reaction would drive them beyond their capacity. Mercy, you are here to learn the origins of our magic, and they are not of this earth. However, we have months to catch you up to speed. This new knowing is only for the ascended. You have begun your process. Some never do. LJ isn't to know anything more than what she is meant to. It's best we keep this to ourselves for now."

As if on cue, the server appeared, ready to take our dinner order. Meanwhile, I was lost in some key references Max made separating earth from our own, inferring otherworldly connections that surprisingly did not seem unfamiliar. As LJ made her way back to the table, I thought about Saturn's Bridge and how I would give anything to be able to process this in my safe cave of comfort. Keep it to ourselves for now? Clearly this concept also ran in the family.

"Looks like you two had an intense conversation. Momma, have we decided to give up healing work for a career with the electric company?" LJ said in a teasing tone. "What's for dinner?"

"We decided to get red beans and rice and Cajun sausage with peppers and onions for the table. Grounding food for Mercy, and fuel for your work night."

The dinner imbued with the richest of Cajun spices proved Max right; it was just what I needed to ground. Laughter quickly found its way back to our circle of three as we spoke about art and love, and I caught them up on life in Appalachia. After the last bite was consumed, we offered our prayers of action to the Source. Unlike other traditions, we expressed our gratitude for nourishment at the end of the meal. The distraction of hunger and the anticipation of conversation sometimes takes the energy from what is known in other spiritual circles as a pre-meal blessing. Our kind, in a state of satisfaction and pleasure, offered words of encouragement and action, along with gratitude for the company, post-meal. Food was nourishment for the body, and the purpose of eating was to keep us fueled up to continue doing the work.

LJ pulled an aragonite earth stone from her backpack. I called in fire to our table candle with the snap of a finger, and Max poured water into a cup. We placed all the items in the center of the table.

Max opened her palms to face the sky, and with all her potency she spoke these sacred words: "Air is in our breath, the earth holds our feet, fire lives inside of us, driving us forward always. Water gives us new eyes with its softness and courage with its slow carve effect of forever changing. It is my sacred prayer that we stand firm in our path, heart and eyes far reaching, open to the moons that birthed us. This meal gave us strength so that we may give back direction. The Stones from the sky with the blessings of our moons will always prevail. Into the shadows we go."

"Into the shadows we go." LJ and I affirmed.

I called a car to take me to meet Abel. As soon as I stepped out on the corner of Royal and Frenchmen, I felt alive, connected to the pulse of the city. Music danced through the streets like a ghost welcoming another aimless wanderer, destined to be an unseen complement to the magic that made this city thrive. I could feel my body shaking, knowing in just a few minutes I would be holding him. I needed this man. Animal magnetism at its maximum level consumed me. My breath started to leave my body as it always did when he was close. Feeling him before seeing him was part of the attraction. It always confirmed my vision of the chord of destiny that sealed our attachment, destined to feed each other in ways that were foreign to traditional lovers. We were not a couple. We were a force existing only in certain moments of life.

I crossed the street, making my way to our favorite bar, and there he stood. As I got closer, he looked at me in that way he always did. Never a man of many words, he stared into me with such longing that with the might of all my intuition, I could not reach him. Yet I submitted willingly to that mystery. Our initial engagements always started with this scan of all the lifetimes we evolved through in the presence of each other's hearts. Between us was a cosmic storm of growth, loss, danger, love, and desire. We were standing there like ravaged animals, waiting for permission from some unseen force to speak or touch. His finger traced a strand of hair away from my cheek. As

I stood, lost in his dark eyes, he leaned into my ear and whispered, "Breathe, Mercy." As life started to return to my body, I felt him press me gently against the wall, hovering too many long, drawn-out seconds, forcing me to linger in that longing before he decided to kiss me. "Welcome home."

I rubbed my hand down his chest, stopping just short of his waist. "When you stare past my eyes, I feel the Universe hold her breath. Saturnali, can you handle me finally existing in the same city as you?" He grabbed my hand and held me close, and we made our way inside to order a drink.

The bar was loud late on this hot summer night. The music playing seemed different than what ordinarily resonated on Frenchmen. I couldn't quite see who it was; the stage was removed from our line of vision. Conversations varying on multiple degrees of energy only intensified our urges. Abel, sensing my distraction, moved closer to me, tracing his finger in gentle circles on my back. "How's Madame Maxine? Still full of hate for me?"

"Stop. She doesn't hate you. They just need time to know you like I do. Let's get to the art market before it closes for the evening. It's a bit calmer on the street."

Frenchmen Street was host to a lovely gathering of local artists where one could find many things saturated in the vibrations buzzing about, a piece of NOLA present in all of them. We grabbed our drinks and walked a few blocks up the street. Abel dominated the conversation relaying increasing tension with his father, a situation that never seemed to change for him. His family had settled in New Orleans in the late 1800s. Existing in that tradition gave him no other option than to uphold the family commitment to the Pythagorean Brotherhood. That restraint almost visibly chained his aura, underscoring his lack of freedom to be something else to the world.

The art market was emptying as vendors were making their way home. Abel started speaking to a local artist about oil paintings. I was drawn to this old magnolia tree in the back. My surroundings grew dim, illuminating just that tree in my vision and the waxing moon cradling the space above. A fragrance permeated the air. It felt familiar, yet I could not quite place it. Curiously, the scent grew stronger the closer I got to the tree. To the left of the tree, an artist's booth displayed carefully crafted wood and metal items, sculptures presenting a reflection of the Universe. Suddenly, a branch from the tree above started to shake as something flew away. Two white feathers floated down, one finding its way to me and the other landing on an item at the end of the table where a woman of remarkable beauty was sitting. I placed the feather in my bag, then quickly made my way to the other one.

The woman stood and grabbed the feather off a wooden spoon I was all too familiar with. "I believe this belongs to you."

As I reached to take the white feather from her, time stopped for a moment and all around me was stilled. The noise of the streets, jazz music, tourists, and cars disappeared from my ears. The Mother of the great wheel of time was capturing this moment.

"That red spoon, is it yours? Is this your art?"

She looked at the moon, then looked at me and said, "Remember."

Time resumed just as Abel was calling my name. I turned around to see him carrying a painting wrapped in brown paper tied with twine.

"Surprise! I wanted to gift you something inspirational for your new home."

As I turned back around, she was gone. Her voice when she spoke to me sounded like it was a thousand years old, the vibration in her tone so distant.

"Did you see where the artist I was speaking to went?"

"What artist? Mercy, there was no one there. I was right across from you the whole time. The gentleman I purchased your gift from even remarked if you were interested in anything to let him know. He was watching that table for another artist."

I wanted to tell him, but his knowledge of magic was minimal. We were healers in his eyes, operating on the same level as his own family.

"You must have overlooked her," I said quickly, dismissing the event. "Let's go to my place."

The impish grin on his face said everything.

"Lead the way, Angel of Mercy."

As we were leaving, I asked the artist Abel referred to about the spoon. "I'm interested in speaking to the vendor attached to that booth with all the metal and wood offerings."

The gentleman replied, "He's a musician playing up the street. I have his price listing. What can I get for you?"

"Oh, that's quite all right. I was hoping to get some details on a specific piece."

"Sure thing, miss. We set up around six in the evening. If you come back tomorrow around that time, you can catch him. His name is Hagan."

I thanked the gentleman, and we left. Abel was focused on driving, dodging the tourists weaving through the busy streets. I was not quite able to shake yet another appearance by the white crow. I'd find Hagan tomorrow. Then there was Her — who was she? I felt her urging me to conjure a memory, but of what? The streets around us grew progressively quieter, all the way into the cottage's narrow alleyway.

We had barely made it through the doorway when Abel pulled my body close and instructed, "Open your gift." I obliged and began unbuttoning his shirt. He picked me up, carried me to the bedroom, and stood over me, staring. He was at once stoic and impassioned, and in these moments, when he could seemingly entertain two conflicting emotions at once, I understood our sacred contract to each other was constantly evolving. We explored each other through the unspoken conversation that metamorphosizes between two bodies. The connection of our souls was so strong we felt the vibrations of anticipation, each able to sense the other's next move. The great hunt of the moon priestess and the scorpion; a pre-war dance of predator and prey, where the roles of each were yet to be decided by the fates. Tortured, we silently begged through every intense second, "Release me." The dance began to slow as the drum rumbled its last warning.

The room was heavy with silence. Our union always ended in this post-war state, where the wounded lay on the battlefield awaiting the blissful transition to eternity. The exchange of each other's darkness in a force of passion burned away the weight of pressure that burdened us both. Sometimes love lifts, elevating you towards soft surrender. Sometimes love sets you free. Freedom is just an escape.

"My father is sending me to Europe in a few days to retrieve artifacts from our office in Budapest."

And there it was, the source of his heavy mood. His voice was full of concern delivering this news.

"Our recent disagreement started from my resistance to accept a promotion to the import division of artifacts for the company. He feels a decade of researching and documenting the rarer pieces for our preservation library is the right amount of experience to travel, investigate, and become a full-time buyer. I have no choice in the matter." He held me close. "Always ships in the night. Seemingly our fate." He ran his fingers through my hair, lost in his own self-doubt.

"Think about all the exciting places you'll see! I have always dreamed of having the life of a traveler, drinking in cultural richness from unfamiliar territory. When I'm faced with a situation that appears out of my control, I try to remove my emotion for just a moment and analyze what I am in control of. You could make another choice, doing something different. The consequence might be losing all ties to how that previous situation adds value or serves you. Or you can go with the flow and look for the adventure in it all."

He stared, annoyed by my positivity.

"Coffee?" I offered, forcing a smile.

I took a quick exit to breathe through this new information, the smell of coffee grounding me away from the pain in my chest. I wanted him to fight for his happiness, but I could not make that decision for him. I could only love him through the process. On the other hand, this would give me time to solve the mystery in my own story.

Abel stood in the door frame between the kitchen and the hallway. My heart burned every time I looked at him. His usual tension was washed away, replaced by calm.

"Open your present before I go."

I pulled the paper off the painting. I stared, unable to move.

"You don't like it." His alarmed tone was no doubt a reaction to my silence.

Van Gogh was responsible for my love of dark landscapes, the ones that have the observer discovering tones of madness, of internal storms birthed through poetic darkness. The mood of this divine work had me drifting to a place far away. My attention was immediately captured by a large oak tree with a web of crooked branches trembling towards a dusky sky. The storm was painted into the scene as though I could smell the season and its harshness as imaginary droplets of rain streaming down my face. The fire in the distance was keeping warm a group of shadowy figures staring desperately toward this god of nature that eerily resembled nature's gallows. This was no Starry Night.

"Mercy, I never meant to make you cry. You have such a love for dark art. I ... I... I'll take it back..."

"No!" I objected. "It reminds me of a familiar truth, the storm inside myself. Abel, it's everything!"

I hugged him as tightly as my gratitude would allow. He returned his affections, kissing me with passionate relief.

"I have a lot of research to catch up on for the next two days before I leave. You should stop by the library tomorrow. I would love to share some discoveries with you. These pieces I have been missioned to retrieve have proven to be quite fascinating. I'm working with members of the brotherhood across the globe on this project. It takes pagan darkness to a whole new level. You will love it! Maybe we can grab lunch afterward? I'd love to hear your thoughts on all of it."

"I am utterly intrigued, Saturnali!"

CHAPTER 3

Uncovering the Past

The moon has a certain charm before dawn. I sat on my porch drinking in her light, a welcome recharge. The warmth in the air promised the thick haze that is summer in New Orleans. The transition from dark to day held magic that was perfect for standing in the realm of the veil, a space where everything unknown finds connection.

Suddenly, a loud crash came from inside the house. I entered the kitchen to discover the painting from Abel, previously leaning against the wall, now lying flat on the other side of the room. I picked it up to examine it for damage, and as I did, I noticed something I hadn't last night — the artist's signature: Hagan. The same artist whose spoon magically stole a moment from me at the art market last night. This further reinforced my need to meet this mystery person.

At 10 a.m., the heat already was delivering warnings of the day ahead. As I drove down the street, shimmers of scorching air rose from the asphalt. The library of the brotherhood was in a warehouse off Canal Street, where the public remained oblivious to a thousand years of artifacts right under their noses. The brotherhood was able to maintain its secrecy under the guise of Apollo Industries, an international company with interests in several lanes of business. Their primary focus, however, was imports and exports. Since 1895, the New Orleans office had been managed by the Saturnali family, the

47

same family who was the original financial investors of the Board of Commissioners of the Port of New Orleans. Abel's father, Victor Saturnali, was not only the owner of Apollo Industries-NOLA Division, but he also sat on a board of spiritual leaders in the community known as the Council of Hidden Saints. Auntie Maxine also was a board member. They guarded the interests of nontraditional spiritualists while also preserving the deep occult foundation on which the city was built.

I pulled into the warehouse where Abel was waiting to take me up to his office. In the three years I had been visiting, he'd never taken me to his family's business. I'd met his parents two years ago, and let's just say they were less than warm.

"Your timing is perfect! I'm in the process of shipping a key piece from the collection."

He eagerly took my hand, guiding me to his office.

"Shipping? I thought you were traveling to collect pieces for this project."

"Oh, I am. However, once I study and document each piece, it isn't stored in the Apollo warehouse. These items are heirlooms to the brotherhood, pieces of our history. They'll be stored in a secret location in Mexico. I can't go into the dark details here. We'll save those for lunch." Abel reached inside a shipping crate, delicately pulling out a box made of dark burnt wood. My body turned cold at the sight of it. The room suddenly smelled like damp earth from deep in an ancient forest. The black velvet inlay of the box cradled some sort of ancient weapon.

Words finding slow passage through the nervous tremor in my jaw, I asked, "Is it a battle ax?"

"It's a ritual butcher's cleaver!" He was beaming. The handle was made from the same burnt wood that constituted the box it rested in. The double-edged steel blade gave off a blue pearlescence in certain light. "The transition element from the handle to the blade is remarkable, bands of stacked rings made from gold, bone, and obsidian. You can feel the intensity of this piece."

My eyes explored the box. "Ritual cleaver, you say? So, this was used for sacrifice. Animal or human?" As my fingertips touched the beautiful bands, my body grew colder. The air retreated from my lungs. Darkness shrouded my consciousness.

My eyes opened slowly to a frantic Abel hovering inches away from my face.

"Are you OK? You fainted!"

Not again. "I haven't eaten today." I blew it off, suppressing the knowledge that this happened to me just days ago. "I am sure food will fix it. Are you still up for lunch?" What is happening to me?

Abel was quiet the entire way to the restaurant. As soon as we were seated, I could tell from the look on his face there was no getting out of a talk addressing his concerns.

"Mercy, you haven't been yourself since you got into town. Is it me? What is going on?"

I grabbed his hand. "I'm just tired, love. Yesterday was a long day." I flashed a reassuring smile. "You have nothing to worry about. I need a few days to adjust to my new environment. Tell me more about your project. I'm excited to hear what's been stealing so much of your time."

To be fair, that was partially true. I wanted to know more about this cleaver. Clearly it held influence over me, and with all signs coming at me loud and clear these days, I needed to know everything he knew.

"A year ago, my father shared a story about our family history. In 1889, a private businessman gave a large cash donation to the Brotherhood in exchange for a task to be completed. This deal would birth my family's current fortunes and create a whole new focus for the Brotherhood, changing its mission forever. Historically, Pythagoreans always researched different avenues of soul evolution, sacred missions, and reincarnation. Great philosophers rooted in mathematic theories proved there is a universe of endless possibilities. We learned that certain people carry higher frequencies, putting them more in tune with the universe. This knowledge found us researching methods to elevate those vibrations, believing we could quicken the journey towards enlightenment; hence, the Brotherhood's collections. And apparently, we are not the only group trying to get hands on these sacred artifacts. There are many, and some have bad intentions. Mercy, I am confiding in you because I don't want to keep things from you. I also hope that you may be able to offer insight into this particular history."

Our server placed our lunch on the table, providing a brief distraction. He took a few bites and continued his story.

"In the early 19th century, a powerful witch and her newborn babe moved to an English country village. She lived on the outskirts toward the woods, keeping mostly to herself. Word of her solitary motherhood carried throughout the village and into neighboring towns, creating concern among religious leaders. They sought the counsel of Priest Liam Thomas Anders. His Swedish grandfather, Hugo Anders, was part of the inquisition and slaughter of the last witch executed in Europe, Anna Goldi, in 1782. Hugo had a large following in the Catholic hierarchy, and his money fed the church, turning the people's eyes away from his dabbling into occult eradication using supernatural weapons. His weapon of choice was called the Amulet of the Sun, a necklace with the eye of Horus carved in obsidian and drawn in amber. This necklace, when given to its victims, rendered them powerless during the full moon of their birth month.

"Liam Anders was in possession of his grandfather's weapon. A secret council formed in the basement of his church. People from communities throughout the countryside met one fateful evening to formulate a plan to kill this powerful witch. Liam instructed the fifty or so villagers to befriend the odd woman, trick her into thinking they needed her wisdom. The necklace would be gifted to her when trust was achieved. Death would be delivered then. The citizens cautiously started getting to know the woman. Time went by. The witch birthed the village's babies, made medicine for the sick and soothed many wounded souls. Her daughter was now six years old, playing with all the other children. The villagers had grown to love them both.

"But not all the council members agreed. The priest, angry, feared his flock had lost its path. He hired a beggar to solicit help from the witch and gave him the necklace to barter for payment. After she provided him with guidance, she walked this man to the edge of the road. He gave her the necklace as payment, encouraging her to put it on. She obliged, and that is when the council grabbed her. Liam knew the child would be left behind. He grabbed the girl and hurried back to the church."

Our meal had come to an end. The story, far from over, was consuming me, every sentence increasing the size of the lump forming in my throat. I took a drink to clear my voice. "She must have been one powerful witch to inspire such a ploy."

He replied, "Of course she was. The ancient witches were the most powerful beings on earth."

"Were, you say? Witches like that don't exist anymore?" I responded, hiding my knowledge with playful banter.

"As time moved on, technology reduced communication between people and nature. Intuitive connection became more about primal survival than spiritual development. Earth became imbalanced. A new world got in the way of the quiet journey to the veil. Eventually, power stopped growing in witches, and the world adapted to a more human way of thriving. Now energy wielding takes the forms that your family practices." My eyes must have doubled in size, because Abel quickly added, "Maxine is open about your family's healing offerings and commitment to helping souls evolve."

A part of me felt guilty for letting Abel remain in ignorance, about magic and about me, when he was clearly opening up to me about his world, but everything he was saying just confirmed that he wasn't in a place to receive the truth.

As we stepped out of the restaurant, I saw my feathered friend perched on a street sign on the corner. When she saw me spot her, the crow flew towards the river. I got into the car and grabbed Abel's hand.

"Do you think we could go to the river? I'd love to hear the rest of the story."
I looked deeply into his eyes, almost daring him to refuse me.

"As you wish, my sweet moon."

We drove a few minutes down the road and parked near the banks of the
Mississippi. The overcast sky added a level of melodrama to the murky river
flow. We found a bench facing the muddy water. I felt her over my shoulder. I
did not need to look; I knew she was there. A caw broke through the silence.
Abel looked to the distance and continued the story.

"Liam rejoined the crowd, and the campaign for her death began. Legend
says her screams drew every crow for miles. She screamed herself into a state
of madness at the separation from her child. She feared for what they might
do to her."

I interrupted him, my voice caught up in panic. "Wait! The daughter. What
did happen to her?" I was so emotionally involved in the tale that tears were
welling up in my eyes at the thought of that soon-to-be-motherless child, but
Abel must not have noticed, because he carried on, ignoring the question.

 "Finally, a woman was permitted to bring her some hot tea. She took one
drink and lost consciousness. The very medicine she'd used in her own healing
practice was now coursing through her body, forcing her submission. She
died that day, hanged in front of all those people she had helped. No one
stopped it. No one."

Involuntarily, I shivered, feeling in my bones the deep sense of loneliness this
woman must have endured.

"I believe what happened is that the people's fear took over," Abel continued. "Liam convinced them that the witch's presence among them meant they had somehow fallen from grace, and the people were frozen by this illusion. Madness drove them to do a deed that couldn't be undone. The writings of Priest Liam Thomas Anders document that, as the witch's body swung from the gallows, a storm moved in, bringing with it a torrent of heartbreak over what had transpired. It was as if the rain washed away the haze of hate that had muddled their minds. Deep in Liam's heart, he wrote, he felt shame."

I stood up, walking to the edge of the rocky bank. "How could they not help her?"

Once again ignoring my question, he walked over to stand beside me, continuing, "So that brings me back to my original story. A businessman offered a very large sum of money to my great-great-grandfather, a leader of the Italian chapter of the Brotherhood, to retrieve the necklace, a job that apparently would involve some dark and dirty work. The task was accepted, though not without hesitation. As is often the case, money made up for the gruesome details of the deal."

Thunder roared in the distance as I turned away from the water, searching for the crow. She hadn't moved from her perch, and she was staring at me with the strength of the mountain that birthed me. I drank in enough of that strength to turn back to Abel and ask, "What happened next?"

He looked back toward the river, not looking at me. "The Brotherhood's search led them to the ritual cleaver you held today. It was the blade that cut the rope that bound the witch's body to the tree. She was laid out in the field, and the storm raged all around the men as they cut her body up, keeping certain parts and burning the rest. Legend says an enormous murder of crows caused an otherworldly commotion, making the task difficult for the men to carry out.

"The businessman told the Brotherhood they would be doing a noble thing, retrieving the necklace to house under their protection. It was then my family learned that ancient objects and beings held more power than they'd initially thought. The witch's body parts, along with the necklace and some of her possessions, were supposed to be sent to different Pythagorean chapters all over the globe, but during transport, a Brother went rogue, stealing most of the items."

I felt numb. I didn't want to hear about this part, so I asked again, "Abel, the girl. What happened to her?" I felt the blood leaving my body as rain began to fall. I began to shake.

"No one knows. Some say she was taken in and raised by a village couple, or she ran away. Liam hanged himself five years later, from the very tree that had birthed his burden, but there are stories that say he raised the child out of guilt until she turned eleven, then gave her all his money, sending her far away to start a new life before taking his own."

Instinct is a powerful protector. I felt like my soul was on autopilot; I had no control of the survival mode awakening within me. Something told me to manage the emotion that was hell-bent on crippling me. I was overwhelmed by rage, sadness, longing, and confusion. It took all my strength to control the storm inside of me.

Abel saved me from having to speak next. "This rain is going to get heavier, and I need to get back to work." He grabbed my hand, leading me back to the car. The crow was no longer in my sight, and suddenly I was consumed by dark, lonely thoughts. The car ride back to Apollo Industries was long and quiet. Abel pulled into the parking lot, shutting off the engine, leaving just the sound of rain on the windshield. "Mercy, I am excited to finally take part in something important on so many levels. I am going to finish my family's original mission."

I was now obsessively motivated to stay close to Abel's work. I nonchalantly asked, "What will you do when you find them all?"

The excitement found its way back to his voice, "Research. My father promised if I completed this mission, I could return back to the library to continue my studies." Eagerly, he looked deep into my eyes. "I know you love a dark mystery. So? Isn't this intriguing?"

"It is unlike anything I have ever heard. I am glad you have passion in your work. May the knowledge gained from your new chapter be applied in the most illuminating ways." The rain had eased up as the sun started to peek through the cloudy sky. I leaned over and kissed his cheek. "Thanks for sharing. I'll call you later."

As soon as I got into my truck, the deep shiver returned to my bones. I felt the urgent need to speak to Maxine, but I arrived home to find she was not there. My nervous system was on overdrive, heightening my senses. What would Mim do? I paced my kitchen floor, wanting to call her. I needed her wisdom and comfort. But I wouldn't worry her. I would put on the tea. That's what she would do.

Perched in the shadows, I witness men hovering like vultures over fresh meat. The rain has softened on the end of a wicked storm into a hypnotic mist. Others work feverishly in the distance, harvesting dry wood for a fire. I can't catch my breath. My body is paralyzed, unable to react to this gruesome unfolding. The butcher is leading this horror, his confidence in the art of dismemberment clearly evident. The sky is illuminated by the glow of a large bonfire. The heat is so intense I can see it in color. I stumble from up high, my fall turning into a glide. I fly closer to the scene. A row of boxes containing human remains lies on the ground awaiting transport. The rest of the body is burning in the fire. The butcher grabs a severed arm and lays it on the flat rock. He raises the blade. I gasp at the sight of his face. Abel? The blade falls violently, severing a finger. I can't breathe. I can't move.

The finger is adorned with a ruby ring.

"Mercy, wake up! Wake up, Mercy!"

I suddenly awoke to LJ shaking the life out of me. Maxine came rushing into the house.

"It flew away." Her voice was full of concern as she looked at LJ.

"Flew away?" I asked in a state of confusion, pain crushing my chest.

"Mercy, we heard you screaming from the main house. Mother looked out the window and saw a white crow perched on your porch. We ran over here immediately. You were having a nightmare."

Shaking, I was suddenly overwhelmed with a wave of nausea. My panicked thoughts replayed the same words over and over in my mind: I'm dead. He killed me. I'm dead. He killed me. I immediately ran to the bathroom. My nerves violently purged everything from my body, and then the world turned black.

I became aware of the sound of a ticking clock, and my eyes opened slowly, taking in the deep purple walls surrounding me. Aunt Maxine's room looked so like Mim's. The nightstand beside the bed displayed a picture of two young sisters during a solstice ritual at Stonehenge in the '70s. Mim had the same picture hanging in her kitchen by the stove. Quickly though, the comforting reminder of home faded away, followed by a flood of confusion and sorrow.

"How are you feeling, Emerson?" Maxine was sitting quietly in a reading chair in the corner of the room.

"Emerson? The only time that name gets used is when I am in serious trouble." I got up and sat in the chair across from her.

"Aren't you? What is going on? I know you are keeping things from me. The white crow is not like anything I have ever sensed. I cannot help you, Mercy, if I don't know what's going on."

"5:30. How is it already 5:30? Max, I promise I will tell you everything tonight. First, I have somewhere I need to be." I had to get to that art market and find Hagan. I knew this stranger held some pieces of my mystery. I could feel it in my bones.

"Are you off to meet Abel?"

"Don't say his name to me right now. If he comes by, do not tell him what happened today. Not one word. I think my life may depend on it." I grabbed my things and made my way to the door. Max stepped in front of me.

"Are you safe?" she asked, in the most collected state. Maxine was one cool drink of magic. She rarely lost her center in any situation. I believe that's what made her the most powerful witch of all.

"I am safe for as long as you keep this to yourself. I am off to follow a lead. As a Stone woman, for moon's sake, one step ahead is my only option. I'll be back in a few hours. I think I will walk to Frenchmen. I could use some fresh air and a moment to collect my thoughts."

"What if you pass out again? I'm not sure going anywhere is a good idea. However, I trust the ascension. LJ's working the early evening shift on Bourbon Street tonight. She will be close in case you need her. Here, take this." She handed me a bracelet. "The belt of Mars came over with our family from the old country. It's made of iron. It awards the wearer the blessings of strength, sharpness, and confidence in power. On your way out, stuff your pockets with yarrow. Stay sharp, Mercy."

Walking in New Orleans was a charge. The city, even in its quiet moments, buzzed energy so powerful you could feel the timelines of old wrapped all around you. Deep down, I knew the dream was more than a dream, but I would not face that right now. My heart raced faster the closer I got. As I turned onto Frenchmen Street, I saw the vendors of the art market setting up. I saw the man with the paintings from the night before setting up his table. The section in the back by the magnolia tree remained empty.

"Excuse me, sir? Can you tell me if Hagan is here?"

He took off his hat, wiping the sweat off his brow, and just as he was about to speak...

"How's it going, Kentucky?"

I spun around to find the one and only Mr. H. Chambers Hoon standing right in front of me.

"Hagan, this young woman has been waiting on you." The man put his hat back on, returning to his setup duties.

"Hagan? Oh, I see, H. Chambers Hoon. You have got to be kidding me."

"Don't look so disappointed, Kentucky. I think we both knew the path would circle us back around to each other." He gestured towards the man working. "Mack said you came here to see me? What's a-matter, kid? You look stunned!" He laughed in a mildly obnoxious way.

I could not speak. I felt the urge to let go, and the darkness started clouding my eyes, when all of a sudden he grabbed me and hugged me tight. I started to sob uncontrollably. I was vulnerable, and this stranger was delivering me the energy I desperately needed. I didn't speak and didn't have to. He held my hand in the most nurturing way, and we walked several blocks in absolute silence. With each step I felt a little more of the heaviness leave. We made our way into a coffee shop. There was a private booth in the back, sectioned off from the main dining area.

Hagan placed a cup in front of me. "White almond Russian, a cup of comfort."

The steam opened my breathing after all that heavy crying, allowing me to continue finding my center. "Who are you to me?" I asked.

"I was vending at a summer festival in north Georgia a few days ago when an old friend paid me a visit. Now, time has taught me to accept what's in front of me when in the presence of this friend. I received an invitation to work in New Orleans and without hesitation made plans to travel this way. Hattiesburg proved once again my feathered friend was leading me to awareness when I saw you eying her at the gas station."

My heart grew warm. "The white crow?"

"The one and only." He smiled, taking a sip of coffee. "What sorrow has you in such a state? What brought you to me?"

The words came pouring out of me with ease and trust. I told him everything that had led up to this moment, everything except the ruby ring. I needed to sit with the fact that it had been in my family for generations. Another mystery. How did we come into possession of that macabre treasure box?

"I feel like I am sitting with a bunch of tiny pieces to a great big puzzle with no box cover to be a guidepost. I would like to know about that painting. What was your inspiration? Who are you to me?"

"The short answer: I don't know. I have been wandering the world with no memory of who I am since the 1890s. I am over a century old, Mercy. You see, I have my own mystery. The white crow started appearing to me, and it was not until many years later I realized she was there to guide me. I think about all the times I was dismissive of her presence. I must have missed so many things. Over time I came to realize that when she appeared, my life seemed to make more sense. My inner witch was never subjected to the sleep that consumed my memories. That part of my life, thankfully, remained preserved, the great knowing that breathes in all of us.

"The painting you received was the piece I created the night before I lost my memory. I awoke the next morning frantically trying to put together the pieces of my life. The first thing I noticed was the paint on the canvas hadn't dried. My motivation for creating it remained unclear. I only knew my name because it was stenciled on my desk and tagged on the art that surrounded me. Since then I've discovered that all my creations prior to memory loss have a secret enhancement. Some of my art contains portals to the space and time of the scene depicted. The common theme hiding behind each door is loss." He stared deep into the distance. We sat in silence for several minutes, his face creating shapes that reflected his sorrowful trip through time. Tilting the cup to swallow every drop, he finished his drink.

Hagan, breaking through his trance, continued, "When you listen to a song that takes you back to a powerful emotion or place in time, or when art moves your soul outside of its shell, that is my magic. A door appears in a chamber of your heart. Inside, the elixir of inspiration pours from the collective well of the muses. Some don't see the door. However, the cravers of internal growth will manifest glorious keys to open those doors, entryways into observing the heart from the inside out. A grand magic, as transforming as it is healing, takes place when they finally walk through. A choice is made to take that inspiration one step forward. It becomes a tool for growth. My art automatically invokes the growth, leaving the observer no choice but to ask why."

Dumbfounded, I stared at him. There was no going back now. I knew in that moment life would continue moving swiftly until this great mystery was fully revealed. I felt the words slowly finding their way to the surface: "I felt our connection in Hattiesburg. And now hearing your story, I feel familiarity so strongly between us. I feel safe with you."

He grabbed my hand. "It's getting late, and I've gotta get back to Frenchmen. You have given my heart much hope, Kentucky."

 As we prepared to part ways, I turned to him. "Thank you, Hagan. Can we meet up in a few days?" My voice was full of hope, where I'd been filled with despair only hours ago. My body filled with relief in this shared unknown between us.

"Of course. I look forward to it," he replied.

After exchanging information, we embraced each other one last time, neither one of us willing to let go. He smelled like a mix of honey and sandalwood. I was suddenly aware of a loneliness that had been present in me since birth. It subtly masked a hunger for my need to know another like me. A small part of this gaping hole was now filled by my new friend in magic. We said our goodbyes, and I made the journey home to tell Maxine everything. I didn't have to do this alone anymore.

The cool night air soothed the storm of visions clouding my mind. A longing for clarity about my newly discovered past life was present in every step on the way home. As I turned the corner onto Dauphine Street, the warmth of community was displayed by people in fellowship on their porches, enjoying the hot summer night. Aunt Max's house was up ahead, nestled in powerful darkness.

The poorly lighted alley behind the house was filled with a spicy aroma. Suddenly, I sensed movement on my porch, forcing my pace to slow in caution. A puff of smoke ascended toward the stars, carrying a scent of deep earth. I was relieved to discover it was not an intruder. Auntie Max sat stoically on the porch smoking her clove. Her weathered hand cradled a fancy cigarette holder made of wood, trimmed in iron. Every finger was heavily decorated by multiple rings. Funny, I am the only Stone woman who does not wear rings. My thoughts turned swiftly to the ruby ring back home. Another subtle movement pulled me back to reality. To Maxine's left, perched on a large chunk of amethyst, was a very contented white crow.

The stars were at their utmost visibility, perfect for storytelling. I took the seat beside Max, the wicker chairs with their plump cushions holding us in supreme comfort. I started from the first encounter with the crow. The story flowed from an unexpected center of reverence inside of me. The ruby ring, dreams, a discovered past, revelations through the eyes of strangers, all pointed fingers at a destiny emerging from my shadow self. A past life. My sweet Abel contributing a karmic mystery all on its own. Madame Maxine Flora Jones, unaffected by the varying levels of drama, soaked in the details as she savored her clove. The only moment her posture became rigid was during my mention of H. Chambers Hoon.

"Long before you ever came into this world, I knew within my lifetime I would see a grand ascension in our bloodline. Something truly magnificent is beginning. I'll call Agatha in the morning. Your feathered friend here has not left my side for some time this evening. I can feel her power, Mercy. She is of a force not of this earth. The hour of rest is upon us. Tomorrow I am speaking at a heritage event in City Park. I expect you to attend as my guest. Some highly evolved people will be sharing their lives' research. We may be able to utilize some of those resources."

She kissed me on the cheek, wishing me a deep healing sleep. In an instant, I could barely hold my eyes open. I stumbled into bed thinking about warmth, the execution of such a notion of hope stemming from Hagan. I was consumed with remembering the touch of his hand. My senses were fully aware of honey and sandalwood permeating the room. The moon hung brightly outside my bedroom window. Surrounded by her light, and the safety of having this new, sweet friend, I drifted peacefully into oblivion.

CHAPTER 4

Red Crow of Justice

New Orleans was a city of wild demons, people distracted in their morning routines, pulsating to a dark yet powerful beat. The drive over to the park was a grand reminder of the magic breathing in these streets. Aunt Maxine had spent the morning on the phone with Aggie. My Mim was calling every ancestor, lighting candles, and burning through countless cups of tea trying to divine wisdom to the latest revelations.

"Thinking about Aggie?" Maxine patted my leg.

"I should have called her this morning. I didn't want to hear the worry in her voice."

"Too late for that, child. Agatha Faye Stone is the great nurturer. She will not rest until we have more clarity on the coming storm. Mercy, try not to worry. We are strong women, capable of handling anything that comes our way. You let today be about absorbing, listening. The Universe is laying this out in front of you. Let it speak."

The sun shining through the passenger-side window cast welcome warmth on my face. The sleep that birthed my morning had a lasting effect of rest on my soul. Art was slung lovingly through the neighborhood, each piece conjured in strategic patterns. We were begged to open, DNA from the great union

66

of the True Mother and the Gods of the Universe more easily spotted in the local inhabitants. Faces of primordial sea gods and goddesses were scattered among Kings and Queens of other realms beyond this earth. This city was alive with vibrations straight from the heart of Gaia.

Our car slowly turned the corner, allowing us the most spectacular view of the park, a deliberate consideration of the holiness of nature's cathedral. City Park is a restorative eye amid the vibrant chaos that surrounds it. Every primal nation has sacred ground at varying points throughout its kingdom; this space we were entering is a gem among the collective of such known sites. Ancient oaks draped the majesty of green held in the landscape ahead of us. One could feel one's own mortality in the presence of something so profoundly old. Some of the trees were nearing one thousand years of age. Oak arms extended like curved ballet dancers, frozen mid-story, only a breath away from the end. Silence only magnified their serene influence. I breathed this in for a minute. That breath touched the strongest parts of my being, reminding me of my newfound power. The driver slowed the car. We arrived at the event just as things were getting started.

Max left me to sit near the stage. She was scheduled to speak early in the program about a charity event hosted by The Council of the Hidden Saints. The Dark Mercury Ball was a fundraiser for the preservation of the City Park gardens. Guests from the magical community would wear unique nontraditional masks that displayed the hidden magic within them, identities tethered to plant magic, sacred animals, or ancient amulets. The average citizen would present the expected Mardi Gras masks of old. It would be an intermingling of decorated beings, marginally hidden. Abel was leaving the day of the ball, and although uncertainty engulfed our partnership, the flame of desire still held steady. The distraction of a magnificent ball filled my thoughts, quieting the worry momentarily. Whatever the past held, it was just that — the past. The present clutched desire in its fists, binding us, connected, to one another, good or bad.

After the announcements were over, the speaker began his welcome. "Heritage is a necessary measure in the evolution of a community toward becoming great. Identity gives us the comfort of knowing where we came from as a city. Certain characteristics of survival are still present in our local citizens. Today we will hear different experts speak about plant medicine and natural healing methods used by this community for centuries."

My thoughts drifted away from the speech as I became distracted by an inspiring scent. A swell of vetiver and sweet tobacco rolled in like an early morning fog, dominating my senses. Suddenly, the speaker closed with these words: "It is my pleasure to introduce world-renowned scholar Dr. Ash Sullivan."

Sharp as a falcon, he locked eyes with me while the audience briefly held its breath. He smiled a quick acknowledgment and leaned deep into speaking on historical bayou healing, specifically the subject of sacrificial possession for soul retrieval, blood journey work. This magic felt good inside of me. I drank every word of the provocative ritual into my own sorceress well. He painted the words inside of me, forcing a soft reveal of power. My blood craved this exchange with nature.

All of a sudden, a tap on my shoulder pulled me out of my daze. "Is this seat taken?"

Ash stood in front of me. Perplexed, I looked at him, and then at the podium, only to find a woman speaking about shade plants. "How are you here? You were just speaking."

He extended his arm. "Let's you and I take a walk, shall we, Emerson?"

I took his offer. We discreetly left the event. Aunt Maxine was invested in the presentation, unaware of my exit. We walked arm-in-arm through the garden over to the grove of oaks that so captured my attention on the way into the park. The fragrance that followed him added an extra layer to the humidity in the air around us. His presence was so engaging, his age indeterminate. Blueish-gray eyes cast a timeless gaze deep into my own, the hue a perfect complement to his vintage Led Zeppelin Swan Song t-shirt.

We stopped at what seemed to be the most noble tree in the grove. "How's your grandmother?"

The words flew furiously from me. "How's my grandmother? You stood in my living room knowing more about me than anyone, including myself!" I screamed toward the sky. "I don't know who I am anymore!" The wind began to blow with such severity I could barely stand. Ash remained unaffected. He raised two fingers to the sky, calming nature in an instant.

He took my hands, delicately responding to my defeat. "Those who wander too far from their center leave a fragile mind. Trauma in the soul is an obstacle course of land mines, a lost highway carrying you far away from the truth. The pain pokes your ribs on repeat. It never stops grating on your nerves until you are forced to make a choice. Weak souls surrender to the annoyance, solidifying their one-way ticket into obscurity. Stubborn souls deny the pain, moving further away from their own power. They create a life of tolerance, settling with less than they deserve. But the strong souls, they face the monster and rip its fucking heart out. They become. Action springs forth evolution. If someone takes your power, you take it the fuck back.

"Birth is painful on levels beyond physical pain. Being abruptly removed from your truth did a number on your mind. An old magic scattered your true self many years ago, throwing fractured pieces so far that Gods and Goddesses from around the universe heard your devastation. Each piece projected an eerie, woeful longing to become whole again. I can't rush your return to self. I can guide, but only you can navigate this discovery, ripping the veil one stitch at a time."

I felt the frailty he spoke of inside myself. I agreed immediate knowing would drive me mad. The crow, Hagan, and Ash all were guides on this journey of slow opening. Somehow, I felt permission to move forward.

"When I was working my healing path in Kentucky, I never consciously acknowledged my longing to evolve towards the Source of what created me. And it was not a Source familiar in the words and beliefs of my surroundings. My true Source was unique. I think when one can be seen as successful in an impoverished community, guilt for wanting more kept me from chasing that dream. Thank you. I feel like I can't say that enough these days. However, you are not a witch. I would feel it. What are you?" We sat on the lush moss at the base of the tree, an inviting pad of green comfort.

Ash leaned back against the old oak, his legs extended, ankles crossed. He closed his eyes and began to speak. "You see this tree? It has witnessed lifetimes of change in the world. Branches decorated with leafy dancers far reaching to the air element. It picks up whispers of goings-on through the shared secrets of words on the winds, a trunk so sturdy providing a bridge, above to below. Its roots are part of an underworld network of ground listeners, the unseen beings who predict the coming of all through the vibrations in surface soil and the earth's core. Imagine all the information this wise one has collected over the years, never having to speak for it, listening to the evolution of life. You ask me what I am. I am many things, Emerson. An enlightened magic being as old as the ground that anchors this very tree. I, too, have collected wisdom over time, encountering different sources of life from this earth and beyond."

His words rolled off his tongue like dark poetry, stealing every gasp from my lungs. "The sacrificial ritual you presented, it spoke to me."

He opened his eyes. With an evil grin, he said, "I was wondering what you heard. Welcome to my gift. It should have spoken to you. It was meant for your ears only. I wasn't part of that presentation. It was an illusion. I have an ability, in anyone's presence, to open my collective wisdom to their deepest desires. Observers have free will and can choose whether they are willing to walk through that door. You, my dear, charged in like a Valkyrie. No shred of hesitation dare be found in your stride. You are starving for answers. But I must caution you. With that, you'll find old enemies waking up." He stood up, offering me a hand. "I sense the presentation is ending. We should be getting back."

As we made our way back, Auntie Max was waiting for me. Before we parted ways, Ash said, "I'll see you at the ball." He kissed my hand and turned to walk away.

"How will I know who you are?" I quickly asked.

Opening his car door, he looked back and answered, "I'll be the brightest light in the room."

I walked over to Aunt Maxine, who had her eyes fixed on Ash driving away.

"And just who is he, Emerson Buckley Stone? I can't get a read on him. I don't trust a hidden being."

"His name is Dr. Ash Sullivan. He is a part of my mystery, Max. We are connected. Just like I am to the crow, Hagan, and Her. I think I am beyond the chosen one for this family, Auntie. I believe I'm part of something that surpasses anything we could ever imagine."

We called a car to take us home. The haze of heat had dampened our clothing, making the air-conditioned car a shock to our systems. Auntie Max said, "Oh, I forgot to mention, Agatha should be landing around eight this evening."

"You forgot to mention! She's flying down here?" I stuttered, my tone at once excited and concerned.

"Mercy, she isn't going to stay away from you after all I shared with her this morning. She booked the first flight out. I have a meeting at the Temples. We are tying up loose ends before tomorrow's ball. I will not be home until ten or after. You'll have to wait for her arrival."

She was excited to see her sister. In truth, I was excited to have another piece of home to tether me down. As soon as the car pulled up to the curb, I noticed Abel sitting on my porch. Maxine, also noticing him, sarcastically said, "Check him for sharp objects." She stepped out of the car. He waved. Maxine returned a nod and walked into her house.

"I told you she hates me!" He laughed, finding humor in her cantankerous ways. As soon as we walked into the house, he pulled me close. "I wish I could take you to the ball. My father is meeting your aunt at the Temples tonight. The family is paying for the venue space as part of their donation. He and my mother are wearing ivory clothing and masks made of laurel and gold. You'll have to be sure and say hello to them."

He began to kiss my neck. Without fail, it was only a matter of minutes anytime we were alone before things quickly moved to physical touch. But a sudden burst of curiosity derailed me, and I pushed away. "Pythagoreans are really into past life theories, right?"

"Of course. The idea of reincarnation, some say, was first proposed by the Pythagorean philosophers. Why do you ask?"

"I think I've stumbled onto some past-life memories." It rolled out of my mouth before I could take it back. "But then again, it's probably just dreams."

He responded thoughtfully. "Dreams could certainly be pieces of past lives. I believe in them but never sought to connect to that part of myself. What are you dreaming about?"

I carefully replied, "They're probably just dreams. What time does your flight leave tomorrow?"

"I have to be at the airport by five. I was hoping to spend the afternoon with you before I go."

He ran his fingers through the long strands of my hair, twirling them around his fingertip when he got toward the end.

Disappointed, I said, "Not tonight. My Aunt Maxine convinced Mim to come down for the ball. She will arrive later."

"Do I get to meet her?"

"I'll have you over for afternoon tea. Her love for that time of day will ease the initial interrogation." I poked him playfully in the ribs.

"I'll text you around eleven before I sneak back in tonight." He leaned into my ear, his breath touching my skin with every exhale. "I'm spending the night with you. It's not an option. I am leaving tomorrow."

"Fine." A smile escaped from the corner of my mouth. It wasn't a hard sell. He knew I wanted him here as much as he insisted on being here. "Be sure to park on the street so you don't wake up the sisters. That's all we need, the wrath of two crones. Moon only knows what danger those two could conjure from a startle."

The morning called me softly before the day found itself present. I sat on my porch drinking tea, listening to Metallica's "Master of Puppets" through headphones. There's something very heavy metal about the sky just before dawn, rising fire burning the night away. That morning was the closest to normal my mornings had been in a while. Abel was sleeping soundly after we spent hours deep in the night worshiping each other, a victim of his own exhaustion. He sold his soul for a night of Pan dominance diluted with reverence and lust. I bought it, exchanging the pleasures of the Moon laced in Hecate. He, like music, was a release for me. Sex and sound. I preferred both experiences dark and primitive.

Suddenly, the large old lavender bush at the edge of the porch began to move. To my surprise, the white crow burst from the middle of it. She circled above my head, landing on the ground in front of the intoxicating plant, then flew back in, disappearing. I didn't hesitate. Headphones still blaring, I stood and walked over to the bush. During my cautious examination of it, I lost my balance.

Everything turned black. The air in my lungs was sucked out in the blink of an eye, replaced with a sweet substance. This newfound breath washed over me, conquering all things human like an intelligent virus. Walls I never knew existed crumbled. Fog encased my comprehension. In a flash, the realization of my new shell found me mid-flight. Red feathers covered me in my magnificent corvid state. I was flying with uninhibited grace, soaring toward a return to the womb of my kind's creation.

I WAS FREE.

There was an awareness housed in this body that gave me immediate notice of my companion flying to my right. The white crow looked at me and said, without words, "Reach deep in your mind to your inner sanctuary, and there I shall reveal myself to you."

A portal sprouted. The exit ramp off this cosmic highway exposed a space near to my heart, my cave. We flew in, settling close to the edge of an underground stream. I was finally on the other side of the Unknown. Across the water stood my beloved rock of many rests, Saturn's Bridge. What I saw in the water enchanted me: myself, for the first time in a long time without my mask. It wasn't the red crow body that mesmerized my inner cauldron; it was the fire in my eyes—a silver flame of home.

"Come out of your shift, child!"

That voice, seasoned with ages of wisdom... I knew that voice. It was Her. The White Crow. The beautiful woman from Frenchmen Street.

"Come out of your shift, child. Don't you know how?"

I realized I didn't know how. She held her arm out, an invitation to perch. I stared deep in her eyes, and she into mine. "Come forth!" she said in a commanding voice.

Metallica returned to my ears as I stood face-to-face with this mystery goddess. I removed my headphones. "I know you, don't I?"

"Indeed, I am the High Queen of the Eastern Realm of Saturn. My name is Esther Cassini. Well, don't just stand there, child. Acknowledge the Queen."

I bowed my head, lowering my station. She smiled, amused at my efforts. Her front tooth had a tiny, dark sparkle in the middle.

"Raise yourself," she commanded. "What is your name?"

"My n-n-name?" I stammered. "My name is Emerson Buckley Stone."

"Is it?" She laughed, walking toward the stream. "Tell me, when I asked you to bring us to your sanctuary, what made you bring us here? You did not choose your home, your family. You chose here. Why?"

"This is home. Well, sort of. This cave is the place I played in as a girl. I can breathe here." I looked towards Saturn's Bridge, and suddenly sadness washed over me in waves. My legs began to shake.

"You are affected by the inevitable, child. Your sorrow will serve you no growth if you hold it all inside. You love this cave because it is like your home. Your true home. You grieve a life that never really belonged to you. Your sorrow has been with you for a while. Today's difference, you are aware of it."

Rage sprung from my tongue. "Don't tell me about my life. You don't know WHO I AM!" The words echoed violently through the cave, shaking the ground so hard that pebbles and dust swirled around us. Surprised by my own power, I took a step back.

Esther laughed. "Calm yourself. Breathe and focus on your heart. Hear its rhythm. Swift pacing is not the heart of a great warrior. Steady yourself."

My heart calmed quickly. "Heart of a warrior? I am no warrior. I am just a helper of humankind, facilitating the evolution of humanity."

"Do you hear yourself? Look, I won't judge your plight; it's rooted in nobility. The warrior and the healer in you are both beings of astounding character. Your stance against me just then, it came from the essence of who you really are: a being of magnificent power. Your voice, barely agitated, moved the earth. Imagine what you are truly capable of. The unveiling must be delicate. Navigating timeline spells are tricky. We've stayed too long. Come, we must return. Fix your shift, child. Will it so. Use your mind. Your first shift was driven by the yearning that consumes you. That feeling is your truth fighting to surface."

Timeline spell?

I could sense a change in the atmosphere and her sense of urgency to leave. She shifted, flying fast and far through the portal. My panic, for once, worked in my favor. The instant my desire to catch up was held in my mind's eye, I shifted instantly. Red feathered majesty had claimed my form, bringing my heart straight back to freedom. I caught up to High Queen Esther just as she was flying though our last portal. She perched on the amethyst on my porch while I, in human form, walked to my door.

"Mercy, I shifted you before arrival. Don't tell anyone, not even your family, about your corvid state. All in good time, child. You have been steady and patient thus far. Don't lose your strategy. Clarity is within reach. I'll see you at the ball."

She disappeared into the morning sky. The experience fed me, leaving me stronger than it had found me. Days ago, I was the woman from an eccentric witchy family in deep Appalachia. Now, I was accelerating towards transcendental destiny. As I turned my attention away from the sky, I felt eyes upon me. The window in the main house perfectly framed my Mim staring down, taking in my exchange.

Abel's car was gone. He had left a message saying he assumed I was out for a run, and he would see me soon. Stepping into Maxine's house transported me back to Mim's kitchen in the hollow. The smell of fresh bread baking washed a sense of home through my being. Maxine stood over a pan of crisp apples and bratwurst. I sat at the table just as Mim made her way down.

"Good morning, sister! Did you sleep kind?" Maxine stirred the sweet mixture, never turning away from the task.

"After a hot bath and your chamomile valerian tea, I was sure I'd joined the dead for a moment. So, yes, sister, I slept more than well."

Mim sat directly across the kitchen table from me. With hard eyes, she said, "You should respect me more than assuming I should have to ask."

Maxine very intentionally sat a cup of coffee in front of Mim. "Aggie, coffee before court, dear."

"We ask a lot of our bodies, this shell which houses our magic essence, the part of us that travels from lifetime to lifetime searching for the whole picture. Food is such a necessary fuel for such an undertaking. This morning a new level of alchemy found its way to my path from my white feathered friend. What you saw, Mim, was my return from my first lesson of awakening."

Searching for answers, Mim looked at Maxine. "The bush, does it lead to an underground cellar or tunnel?"

Maxine laughed. "Nothing in this part of the city is buried deep enough to hold a space of that size."

"It was a portal," I quietly interjected.

Maxine replied, "A portal to where, Mercy?"

"To another place. My lifetimes are lining up for the next phase of my existence. My homeland is calling me." I took a sip of tea and continued, "The white crow is my Queen. Or at least I believe she is. High Queen Esther Cassini of Saturn's Eastern Realm. You both keep referring to this experience as the ascension. I believe it's more of an awakening. The uncovering has begun. I suspect we are all players contributing to this mystery. I stepped through the portal and found myself in the cave I cling to back home in Kentucky. Mim, do you remember when you first took me to the cave when I was a little girl?"

"I remember it well. You came home from elementary school crying. The local preacher's son called you a sinner. He said you and your family would burn in hell for all of eternity. I got a call from the principal saying you punched a classmate in the nose." She laughed and looked at Maxine. "At age six. Can you imagine? Our little Emerson was destined to be a warrior. You cried the whole way home that day. You weren't angry. You were upset over hurting him. I took you to the cave, and all your little emotions were neutralized."

I felt a tear roll down my cheek. "It was there you gave me my first real lesson on being an intuitive steward of the earth, on the importance of many paths versus my path being the only way. It was the start of my foundation, acknowledging the power I come from along with encouragement to surrender to the unknown." My head bowed. "I had forgotten about that day."

"Of course your first lesson with this being would occur in the cave. Every moment we spent exploring that mountain and cave, you always drew watchers. I felt their presence around you always. This Queen will need to meet with Maxine and myself. I won't allow this to go any further without feeling this out in person."

"Watchers?"

"The watchers are spiritual guardians. If you choose to participate with them, your evolution has no limits. If you don't, you stay stuck on the inside like most human beings, consumed by the stillness of complex emotions and sorrow and fear. Action, participation in your own story takes courage. Action evolves you through many life experiences as a soul. Action draws the elevated souls working from the other side to you, to be guides."

She and Maxine were quite different magic beings but equally powerful. If life were a circle, she stood outside of it, observing from a distance. Mim was connected to nature, the elements and futures, the journey. Maxine found her gifts inside the circle. She was rooted in the now, shifting the atmosphere to be more seen by the seekers and hidden from the manipulators. "Mim, Maxine has already met the Queen in her shift."

Maxine looked at Mim. "Aggie, she feels ancient, powerful, yet not threatening. However, I agree. Mercy, I would like to see her once the ball is behind us. We have a busy day today."

"Yeah, about that," I nervously replied. "Abel would like to stop by for afternoon tea. He's never met Mim before and expressed an interest in getting to know the family more."

The sisters looked at each other, obviously wordlessly communicating some secret. Mim replied, "The tea is on for 1 p.m. He is to be not even a second late, Mercy."

Maxine laughed at her sister's stern tone. "I think I'll let Aggie handle this meeting. I have several irons in the fire, and besides, I plan on delivering my own level of royalty in my dress tonight. Sister, feel out his knowledge regarding the past."

The afternoon came quickly. A knock at the door quickened my heartbeat. He walked in with his usual dark energy, heavy served with a side of playful challenge.

"You look beautiful," he said, amused at the sight of giant curlers slung throughout my long dark hair. "I am sorry I won't make the ball."

He kissed my cheek, bringing a small tear to the surface. My words poured out, aching with emotion. "You will have such an adventure. Think of all the stories you will collect to share with me when you return. Abel, I'll miss you. When you return, I'd like to…"

He interrupted, "You make me believe in deeper magic. The air around us is intoxicating, blinding us to anything outside of destiny's plans for us. I love your reflection on troubles I've thrown your way. Physically, we forever find these Kali-Shiva moments with each other. The pursuit of this upcoming adventure, combined with your intuitive nature… We can gain so much. Together we could be so powerful, treasures elevating us both to a higher vibration. We can help so many people."

"Power isn't for everyone."

He looked at me, surprised that I questioned his motives, and said, "What do you mean? Power puts us in a position to be in control of our desire. This will not only change my family's future, but it'll deepen work started by the Pythagorean followers of ancient times. More importantly, it's paving a way for our future. The world needs people like us, Mercy. We heal the broken and balance the lost followers of man."

"As Lord Acton so wisely said, 'Power tends to corrupt; absolute power corrupts absolutely.' You are speaking about power that exists in treasures, knowledge, or acknowledgments. True power isn't what you think or own. True power lies in what your heart decides to act on, inner understanding rooted in self-love and giving."

Subtle differences in spiritual philosophies contributed a rich layer to the foundation of our relationship. Our common thread, a passion for pushing our potential as hard as it could go, was the thread binding us together. We made our way to Maxine's. As soon as we walked into the kitchen, I noticed the regular teacups hadn't quite made it to the table. Before I could say anything, Mim reached for Abel's hand.

"Well, young man, I'm Agatha Faye Stone. You may call me Aggie. Please have a seat. Let's have a chat over some leaves. Does that sound all right with you?" Mim handed Abel a fresh cup of black tea.

"Nice to meet you, Aggie. That sounds fine. Mercy has told me so much about you and the mountain." He took a seat across from Mim. "My name is Abel Saturnali." His countenance reflected slight discomfort to the interrogation energy surrounding him.

"Calm," she commanded. Her power led the direction of our gathering into a sacred space. "The tea will help. It's a special blend I picked up from a stranger passing through the mountain. So, Abel, tell me, what it is about my Emerson that you find so captivating?"

"Mim! Abel, you don't have to answer that question." She put her finger up high, silencing me. Abel didn't quite seem himself. "You spelled him!" I felt the heat in my face.

She pulled me aside. "It's regular tea. The teacup is made from special clay and sapphire from Kashmir. It is spelled to promote truth. Your Aunt Maxine has quite the collection of magical items, including the belt of Mars bracelet around your arm. Now, Abel, where were we?"

He cleared his throat and began to speak. "I have lived my whole life trying to measure up to my family's expectations. That all changed the day I met Mercy in a rare empty French Quarter three years ago."

She leaned in closer. "Who is Emerson, really? What do you know of her past?"

"I don't know what you mean. She's Emerson Buckley Stone from Boone, Kentucky. I never saw myself settling down. Independence is something I deeply value. But there is something about my angel of Mercy. We are drawn together, forced to be in each other's lives." He began clearing his throat.

Mim nodded her head in approval. "Well, looks like you're down to the last sip. Time to swirl!"

Abel placed the cup upside down on the saucer. "Aggie, thank you so much for sharing your talents with me. I can't wait to see what your wisdom holds."

Abel was suddenly himself again. Aggie picked up the cup and began, "I see a circle beside a tree with roots. Your family has cast a blanket of protection around you. I see a dagger with wings. Your great battle will be over knowledge, a war of who is right and who's wrong. I see an open window. This highlights your upcoming travel. Now, if you would, draw a card."

He drew the Nine of Swords. Mim and I looked at each other, and I found myself wondering how she would spin this message.

"This card is a warning. It encourages you to stay flexible and open. Obsession can manifest a single-minded approach to evolution. It says success is not getting to the finish line as fast as you can. They say the devil is in the details. The details of how you walk that path will garner more power and success than the need to be first or right." She took a sip of tea, observing the worry on his face. "Come, now, you must know there's no such thing as a bad reading. Divination provides us with tools to look at our surroundings constructively. All of the cards provide you with lessons to equip you with growth beyond your wildest dreams. It cannot be endless good cards any more than endless good days. Life is a series of ups and downs, guided by choices we make every single second. Make good choices, and you will surely be just fine."

Smiling, Abel replied, "Thank you for sharing this with me. I see where Mercy gets her gift of healing words." He turned to me, and I knew it was time to say goodbye. Mim, sensing my sadness, excused herself to get ready for the busy night ahead.

"Mr. Saturnali, such a pleasure meeting you. May your travel be easy and safe." As she walked away, she said sweetly, "And remember, make good choices."

I walked Abel to his car. "She means well," I said, not knowing how this experience affected him.

He laughed. "I think it's her job to show me how protective she is of you. She was everything I had imagined. Unlike Maxine, I think she may not want to kill me." His grin pushed his dark brown eyes into a playful squint, Pan presenting through human flesh. And there I stood in awe of the pull between us.

We said our goodbyes like lovers do. There was no element of traditional partnership; time hadn't afforded us many opportunities to foster that. We stayed in the underground of our sacred temple, communicating with the elements through physical exchange. My fiery ache for the release I'd become accustomed to illuminated my truth about him and me.

Walking back to my house, I shook the heavy emotions from my mind. Something came over me, and I felt the urge to run. I ran to the lavender bush, diving headfirst into a tunnel of cosmic lush. My shift came quickly as the portal to my cave received me. I flew over Saturn's Bridge, pushing beyond the cave's entrance. Out I flew, fearlessly, into the great wide open.

The midday sun scattered beams of light through the ancient trees of the Appalachian Forest. My red wings revealed their iridescence as they swooped in and out of nature's illumination. I found myself on Mim's back porch. I rapidly shifted and went inside, heading to a secret hiding place to retrieve the key. My body was not quite on autopilot, but a higher part of myself was driving every movement. Giving off an enchanting light, the box called to me as if it were linked to my own consciousness.

Carefully, I removed the ruby ring, placing it on my own hand. The lifeless finger stoked a deep memory, an image of my eyes watching that finger trace instructions while reading from an ancient book. A glimpse into my former life. My former life... The thought immediately presented a portal, presumably to that very world. I knew I dared not go. I returned the box to the mantle with the finger still safely locked inside.

The ring sent a stream of intensity throughout my body. The door opened, allowing my effortless shift to fly high into the sky. I headed straight for the cave, anxious to make my return. Flying hard and fast, I returned from the bush. As I landed on the bottom step, I realized I was still in my shift. After I spent ten minutes in contemplation, High Queen Esther came to my rescue.

"Mercy, you cannot jump into your shift on your own. There is an art to managing your soul in both forms. When you shift, you alert other magical beings of your presence, beings you may not necessarily wish to alert."

"I'm sorry!" Her disappointment was written all over her face. "Instinct took over, and I needed to fly."

"Mercy, no more shifting! Your episode pulled me away from important work. Stay out of trouble. That's an order. I've left a gift for you on the bed."

In an instant, she found her shift, the door opened, and off she flew. On the bed there was a gold box with a note: "To Red Crow of Justice, from White Crow of the Eastern Realm of Wisdom. A gift for the ball. Your mask of truth. Open upon arrival."

CHAPTER 5

Masks

In the distance, a violin sent reverbs of enchantment into the evening sky. The intoxicating heart song summoned us to what was sure to be a night to remember. The sound of hooves clacking joined in perfect time, stomping the pavement, matching my every heartbeat. A black carriage of blood moon witches draped in varying shades of red was drawn by two horse—one silver, the other white—stunning onlookers at every pass. Madame Maxine Flora Jones, hostess of such a grand gathering, wouldn't arrive any other way.

The Louisiana heat demanded we make considerate wardrobe choices for this evening's ball. LJ wore a red silk slip dress. The sisters cloaked themselves in elegant red chiffon jumpsuits. Being women of a certain age, they reveled in not wearing dresses to a formal event. "We women of the wild celebrate our form," Maxine stated. "Besides, skin is the only true thing between us and Spirit. We aren't afraid to expose a little skin and buck formal traditions." Our family masks were made of fine black silk, the edges trimmed in tiny rubies shaped like drops of blood. I stared at the gold box containing my mystery mask lying between my feet.

My dress was a vintage deep-red satin that I found at a costume shop in the Quarter, a halter-style dream that confidently hugged every curve. Backless, it plunged into a deep V. The dress transitioned from solid satin to sheer past my hips, cascading into just the right amount of fabric flow for a small train.

Elaborate beads of red and gold created crescent moon shapes scattered gently throughout the sheer bottom. I imagined the crescent shapes glowing.

The sound of the violin grew louder as we drew closer to the ball. I found myself drifting, transported back to a past memory not known in this lifetime.

I am standing at the edge of a forest in the middle of night. An earthy smell of post-rain bliss lingers in the air. The full moon shines so low, it's as if it could crash into the ground at any moment. In the distance, a violin plays as I dance naked under the stars. I am shamelessly lost in joy, drizzled in pure peace.

"Mercy! Earth to Emerson, where are you?"

I came out of my daze to find an overly excited LJ hovering over my face.

"We're almost there, cousin! All the dancing, beautiful people, and the spirits! Let's not forget the spirits! Otherworldly and liquid! I can't wait to see this mystery mask you are keeping from us all. I have secrets too, cousin." She laughed excitedly. "I've prepared a bit of a surprise for all of you, in fact."

She, lover of humanity and bringer of joy, had no knowledge of the weight I was carrying. I admired her ability to constantly hold that "in the moment" space.

Maxine swiftly turned her attention to our conversation. "A surprise? Louisa Mae, you know how I feel about surprises."

"Mother, you will adore it!" Her mischievous laugh was so infectious it made all of us smile. "We're almost there, ladies!"

It was time for the reveal. I opened the box and found myself unable to breathe for a moment. I knew once the sisters saw what lay before me, they would know my new truth. A crow skull fashioned from bits of bone stared back at me, projecting a century's worth of regal power. The seams within the mosaic bone were fused by liquid gold, creating shattered lines across its surface. At the top left side of the mask, a massive plume of red luminescent crow feathers was meant to rest softly against my black wavy hair. In the bottom of the box were two gold armbands.

"Well, let's see!" Mim said.

The mask covered my face from my hairline to the tip of my nose. I was unable to gauge their reaction. However, Maxine, for once, showed a small hint of emotion. She tapped her cane gently on the carriage floor. "Oh, now I understand. The great red crow." She grabbed her sister's hand.

"Red crow! Ooh-la-la! I like, Mercy!" LJ was oblivious to the truth. Doing what she does best, she lightened a profoundly serious mood.

Mim whispered in my ear, "White crow, red crow, so many unknowns. You may be discovering a new chapter; just don't forget your heart. It holds the truths of every lifetime." She hugged me. "Oh, by the way, don't forget your gold bands."

I examined them more closely. A small electrical current ran through each band. "Mim, I think I'll stay out here and breathe for a second. You go ahead. I'll be right behind you." I sensed her worry as I watched her walk toward the entrance.

Most of the guests had arrived. The violin and its wondrous soul strings were now joined by an accordion that exhaled intrigue from every collapse. On each arm I placed a gold band. The electrical pulse intensified, and suddenly an armor of slick red feathers appeared from the gold band resting above my elbow, all the way down to my wrist. I reached into my clutch and removed the final piece of my presentation, the ruby ring. As soon as I slipped it on my finger, everything changed forever.

A gas lantern flickered on each side of the entrance to the ball. Just before I stepped through the entryway, a hand softly touched my shoulder from behind. I turned to find Queen Esther wearing a flowing black strapless dress. She wore a white satin choker and arm bands just like mine but producing white feathers instead of red. Her mask, also like mine, was a crow skull made from obsidian trimmed in white feathers.

"My Queen, you look stunning." I bowed my head respectfully.

"I am a Queen, but not necessarily your Queen. I appreciate your respect, but for now let's stand equally in our power. The Red Crow of Justice is beyond royal titles. You, my dear, are revered and even feared by beings all throughout the Universe. Tonight will be your last night in New Orleans."

"Red Crow of Justice? I'm not ready to go." My heart sank as fear crept in. I wasn't ready to leave the safety net of family.

"All humans go through a process of truth seeking. Bringers of magic just do it more dramatically. All beings in the Universe must suffer the pain of loss or letting go to uncover the truth that exists inside their core. See your fear, welcome it, but lend it no energy to become an obstacle." She circled around me, taking in my presence. "My, my, my, you look magnificent."

"Esther, is that a tear?" I was shocked to see her overcome with emotion.

"Don't be silly, dear. I don't cry." She laughed, regaining control. "Let's meet your family, shall we?"

Side by side, we slowly approached the entryway. The music stopped as soon as we stepped into the ballroom. The whole room gasped at the sight of us. Some guests whispered to each other; others were wide-eyed and speechless.

"Esther, why are they staring?" I had no sooner gotten the words out when I noticed our image in a mirror across the dance floor. The gold seams in my mask, along with the crescent moons etched into my dress, were glimmering with an illumination equal to the moon. Our feathers delivered a prism effect in the lighting surrounding us. Esther's obsidian crow mask left no one to question her rank among the lot. She carried herself like a Queen.

We made our way over to the sisters. "This is my grandmother, Agatha Faye Stone, and her sister, my great-aunt Madame Maxine Flora Jones."

"The Stone sisters. You two left quite the impression at the Stonehenge summer solstice in 1979." The sisters were struck silent by the comment.

"Mim, Maxine, it is my honor to introduce you to High Queen Esther Cassini of Saturn's Eastern Realm."

Esther shook Mim's hand. "Please, call me Esther."

Mim, still slightly stunned, replied, "Very nice to meet you, Esther. Please call me Aggie." She then replaced the welcoming tone with a firm parental one, adding, "We will revisit your Stonehenge impression another time, but for now, Mercy, LJ is about to reveal her surprise."

The lights dimmed, leaving only a single spotlight. In the dark hush, a toy piano began playing a soft, hypnotic melody as two red silk pieces of fabric dropped from the ceiling. Suddenly, the spotlight dimmed as the lights came up to a soft orange glow. In their beautiful hue was a cast of children in varying still poses. That sweet violin tiptoed its way into the scene, complementing the piano in a way equally curious and mesmerizing. Children began to dance ritualistically in reverent joy. Every audience member was entranced. As the tempo rose, LJ appeared at the bottom of the silk fabric.

We stood in awe as she climbed and twisted the fabric around herself. The music behind her carefully framed her aerial dance. The toy piano became quiet as the violin dramatically slowed to longer draws of the bow. LJ was as high as the ceiling when the music abruptly stopped. The spotlight turned red, allowing the shadow on the wall to present the illusion of a red full moon. The fabric gave, and LJ fell like a graceful bird in flight, stopping just short of the hard floor a death-drop illusion meant to steal our breath. The crowd sighed in relief, then erupted in cheers.

A hush fell over the crowd when the violin's slow draw crept back to our ears. From the corner behind the stage emerged a man. He was wearing white pants and a white brocade vest with no shirt. A stag mask with majestic antlers made of selenite covered the top half of his head. This man, although hidden, oozed charm with his dark hair and chiseled form. The great white ghost deer. With hollow eyes, he carried a torch in his left hand, displaying a small flame. The children circled this creature-man. Their faces reflected high excitement, an indication that they knew what was coming next. He tilted his chin towards the sky and breathed a majestic stream of fire. On his third round, the flame turned to a bright cool white and disappeared in a flash.

The white stag took a bow, and applause thundered from the crowd. The house lights came up, cuing the music to return to its full masquerade glory. Couples had begun to make their way out to the floor when the man in white set his sights on me. He walked straight to me and, without saying one word, offered me his hand.

I obliged, and he instantly twirled me around, picking up the dance pace. Off we went, swaying to the rhythm of the gothic orchestra.

Staring deep into the void that would be his eyes, I asked, "What's your name, bringer of white fire?"

He didn't answer. Instead, we melted further into the movement, and vetiver took over my senses.

"Does that answer your question, Red Crow?" His laugh was the same as it was the first day I met him in Mim's house.

"Why, Mr. Sullivan, you certainly were the brightest light in the room."

He pulled me close. "You're in danger, little warrior. The Saturnali family has been asking nomad mages questions regarding your family's origin. They are after an item in Budapest known as the Sword of Atonement. Once obtained, this bringer of death awards the bearer many great advantages over his or her chosen mark."

My mind raced to Abel. "Why am I in danger, and what does my family have to do with this sword? Ash, Abel's en route to Budapest to acquire an artifact. What if it's too late?"

"You're in danger because of who you really are, Red Crow of Justice. Your family is connected to you in ways beyond your current understanding. Thanks to your Pythagorean lover, this artifact is no longer cloaked. Mercy, it is particularly important that you speak to the Saturnali family this evening."

"I'm confused. If I'm in danger, possibly by their own hands, then why would I do that?"

"Little Warrior, I will teach you something you taught me a long time ago. Your enemy will assume they've bested you if you remain ignorant to their treachery. You will be so blissfully unaware in their presence it will keep you close enough to insert your own tactics. Always keep your enemies close."

The violinist left the small orchestra to play among the crowd. In a gray velvet masquerade mask with two small horns made of iron, he walked slowly by us. We briefly locked eyes in a moment of recognition before he continued making his rounds. Hagan?

"May I cut in?" Esther kissed Ash softly on his cheek.

"You two know each other? Of course you do." A tinge of sarcasm seeped into my words.

"Dr. Sullivan is a student, friend, and great love of mine." Esther's eyes stared deep into the void of his mask. "Ash has been an ally to all of us for centuries. In fact, you brought him to the Rings many moons ago and introduced the two of us. Enjoy your family tonight, dear. Aggie and Maxine have been briefed on my plans for you. I have their full support. We leave at 0300. The time has come to undo your confusion."

Intensity consumed their connection, and they all but devoured each other through movement befitting of divine beings. They danced as if each step created new worlds throughout the universe. My heart stung a bit as I realized that I've never known that level of passion.

"Emerson Stone?"

I turned, arriving face to face with Abel's father, Victor. As he had opted for a crown of laurel leaves instead of a mask, his face was fully exposed. "Mr. Saturnali, so very nice to see you, sir."

"Abel should be arriving in Budapest within the next few hours. Pity he couldn't escort you to this wonderful event of the summer. Your Aunt Maxine put quite the time into creating such a lovely gathering, and for such a good cause."

Small talk. Oh, how I hate it, the atmosphere created when one wants to ease into true intentions. I smiled. "She enjoys contributing to any platform that brings likeminded folks together, especially if that event is a charity dedicated to the preservation of nature." I noticed Esther and Ash were watching from across the room. "Abel is so lucky he gets to experience such a trip. You must be so proud of his passion!"

He raised an eyebrow. "Tell me, Emerson, has he shared with you why he's going?"

Apparently, I thought to myself, this is the part where he does a terrible job fishing for information. "He sure has!" I said, enthusiastically. "Abel told me all about being promoted to purchasing. A change of scenery is good for anyone, yeah?" My careless laugh lifted into the air, my small effort to seem not to be invested in the matter.

"Would you like to dance?" I bowed my head humbly before him.

"I'd be honored, Emerson."

He held me uncomfortably close as we began our dance. "You're a unique woman, Ms. Stone. Considering your move, I assume you will be seeing a whole lot more of my son. You should come over for tea soon. I think it's time we get to know each other better."

"I look forward to it." We danced in silence for the remainder of the song. As the melody ended, I delivered the sweetest, most innocent smile I could muster. "Thank you for the dance, Mr. Saturnali."

"My pleasure." His tone carried an air of arrogance. He began to walk away, then suddenly turned to me. "One more thing. Your costume. I see your mask isn't in line with your family's. I'm curious to know the story behind your rebellious choice."

"Rebellious, yes. Well, you see..." As I was struggling for words, Esther interrupted.

"I don't believe we've met. I'm Esther, Emerson's cousin." She stepped into the conversation with the power of the ocean. Her energy rippled like waves crashing into us.

"Cousin?" he replied, sharply. "Emerson, it would seem your whole family is in town."

"Oh, not quite." Esther's presence delivered control and strength. "There's more of us than you can imagine."

His forced smile barely manipulated the contour of his lips. "Enjoy your evening. And Mercy, you should stop by the office for tea next week."

As he walked away, Esther remarked, "He knows something, but not everything." Then she noticed Ash was finding joy with a new partner on the dance floor. "Look at those two. I'm sure she's asking him every question under the moon."

"Esther, Ash said my family is in grave danger. Mim..."

"Aggie was different than the rest of your lot. Her magic breathes from the earth. She is pure of heart, a true daughter of Earth's moon. It's a special magic she has, Mercy. The witches of Earth aren't overwhelmed by the frequencies outside of the atmosphere. Your awakening has indeed put her in danger. You possess a presence that isn't designed to thrive on this planet. Unlike Aggie, you are ancient of the Universe. There are many beings who'd love to siphon your essence." She hugged me. "Looks like things are winding down. I'll see you at the witching hour before we make our journey."

Esther and Ash said their goodbyes to the sisters as the orchestra prepared one last story. A cello delivered a haunting texture that fostered deep reflection. My heart crept into my throat. The solo channeling through this big stringed instrument reached gloriously into the sky, then waned. Softly, a piano began the first notes of Beethoven's "Moonlight Sonata." My heart was heavy. My throat ached with fear. Then...

"May I have this last dance, miss?"

The voice that called from behind sent warmth through my soul. I turned around to find the master violinist hidden in layers of gray.

I placed my hand immediately on his heart. "Hagan!"

He touched my waist. "Interesting circle of friends, Kentucky. I assume your white feathered friend is our infamous guardian crow?" His sky-blue eyes, holding unwavering strength and courage, found the loneliest parts of my being so easily.

"Indeed, it was Her. The quickening pace of this unfolding has left me with even more experiences than the last time we spoke. You should have revealed yourself sooner. I could have introduced the two of you formally."

We circled through the remaining couples occupying the dance floor. He was silent for a few moments. In the air around us, honey and sandalwood lingered like sage cleansing a complicated space. The expression on his face gave a hint of complete connection to the music. He leaned in, telling me, "Since Hattiesburg, I've felt the need to stay close to you. Only you. And for the sake of being even more transparent, I think we need each other. My strength elevates when we're together. Mercy, you have brought me hope. Our white crow seems to be focused solely on you. I'll hang back in the shadow and observe until the moment feels right to expose my own mystery. Your story is meant to unfold in this way. Mine will continue finding its own reveal."

The music proceeded to its dramatic final notes. The song left an eerie foreshadowing in the air. He leaned in and gently rested the bridge of his nose on mine. We embraced each other like long-lost family, finding comfort in our closeness and stillness. Out of the corner of my eye, I saw the sisters watching my moment with this stranger.

"Come home with me." I scrambled, then quickly rephrased, "What I meant to say is, I'm leaving New Orleans in five hours. And at this rate, I have no expectations regarding what's to come. You need to know everything." I felt my cheeks flush. "Bring your violin!"

"Leave me your address. As soon as I wrap up a few things here, I'll be right over."

The sisters quickly tabled their curiosity about the stranger in gray. Traditional concern had no place in this family dynamic. It was understood, more so recently, that life was presenting a magical pathway, a quest that was out of all our hands.

The ball was a success, raising $10,000 more than its initial goal. It was time to walk away from this strange yet beautiful evening. LJ hugged us all before her escape to work. I held on a little tighter, knowing she was unaware of my travel plans. Aggie stopped cold before she got into the car Maxine had arranged to drive us home. "All I ask of you is, whatever happens, stay connected to family, Emerson. You may come from a whole other life, another world even, but this life is yours, too."

We sat on the porch, gazing at the stars peeking in and out of a hazy humid sky. Maxine was inside, putting on the tea. Mim and I sat on the steps, holding hands. "Mim, do you remember when I would stay with you when I was young? I was always plagued with nightmares or dreams so heavy I could not comprehend them. You would wake me up with hot tea. It was as if you anticipated my unrest. We'd hold hands just like this, and the waters would calm in an instant." I stared into the sky. Grief briefly washed over me. "Mim, do you think Abel knows about me? I want to believe he's innocent. I want to believe he's just another soul possibly lost in a new lifetime."

"My sweet girl, any fear I may have regarding your lover, your new support system, or the universe's new journey that's been gifted is canceled by my faith in your purpose. I trust you, Emerson. My intuition may not be on an otherworldly level, but I know enough to feel the strength in you is more magnificent than in any being I've ever known." Her faith in me was all I needed to believe in my ability to navigate things to come. "Settle your assumptions now, Mercy, and focus on what is actively happening. React appropriately when necessary, and always listen to your heart."

As surely as I knew the darkness was coming, I was just as certain that something deep within me was born to charge courageously into that shadow. Suddenly, I felt nauseated. My ears became consumed with the sound of high-frequency buzzing. I was disoriented, feeling like I might faint, when quite the opposite happened. Instead of falling to the ground, I stood up and felt my body trying to shift. As the world faded into a spectrum of fast-moving color, a single touch brought me back to reality. I came to, realizing I was standing in the driveway leading to my cottage behind the main house. The hand pressed against my heart, my saving grace, was that of H. Chambers Hoon.

"Young man, get your hand off of my granddaughter." Aggie's tone showed no tolerance for this strange man pulling me from my trance.

I put my hand over his and held it close. "It's OK, Mim."

"Well, no one invited me to the private driveway meeting." Auntie Max stood in her nightgown, cane at the ready in case violence revealed an opportunity to use it. "Madame Maxine Flora Jones. And you are?"

"Hagan Chambers Hoon, Madame." He looked back to Mim. "You don't remember me, do you?"

She stared for a moment; then, recognition washed over her face. "It can't be! How? You haven't aged a day. It's been thirty years."

I interjected, "I guess I'm not surprised, but humor me. Exactly how is it you two know each other?"

Mim moved Hagan's hand from mine to hers. She smiled and said, "This young man sold me my favorite cooking spoon. Its enchantment reveals itself with every turn. That spoon allows me to stir a pot of anything into my own crystal ball of visions of the future, a true conjurer's spoon. Your energy is sweet and brave. I've never forgotten."

"I never knew your spoon did that, Mim!" It felt oddly reassuring to know she had secrets all her own.

Hagan bowed his head in gratitude. "When I first saw you at the ball, I couldn't help but smile. The memory of you has stuck with me as well. You indulged my enthusiasm for creating art with intention from special materials. Your presence had me in such a divine space, it was like speaking to a vessel for this very earth."

He looked at me, and I knew exactly what he was feeling. Our time of knowing thus far had been short in this lifetime, but I knew him. I KNEW HIM. He was relieved not to be alone anymore. The silence brought the reality of the next few hours to the forefront. I was leaving soon.

"Pull from your strength, sister." Maxine sensed the sadness surfacing in her sister. "She will be back. I'm certain. Hagan, I suspect you'll be sticking around New Orleans. I must insist my sister stay close to me, delaying her travel back to the mountain. You will come over every day at 11:33 a.m. for tea. I'd like for you to occupy the cottage in Mercy's absence. We're going to need to stick together, since clearly we're all in this together."

He knew better than to tell her no. I was glad he would be there for them, and they for him.

"Why 11:33 a.m., Max?"

"Mercy, you can't have all the mystery. I trust you'll maintain a modicum of respect towards your elders and just give an old gal permission to cling to her own mysteries." She winked and made her way back to her house. Without turning around, she said, "Sister, make your goodbye quick. You will need your rest. We have much to do in the coming days." Her cane clacked on the ground as she walked away, reminding me that time was running out.

Aggie hugged Hagan. She then turned to me. "Whenever you need me, just close your eyes and think of my kitchen. I'll be with you in spirit."

We entered the house just as the clock struck midnight. Hagan stopped at his painting hanging on my wall, his body heavy with wonder. I came closer to comfort him when suddenly I started getting nauseated again.

"It's happening again." I reached for him. As soon as he grabbed my hand, the buzzing came back to our ears. In seconds we were in a kaleidoscope of color being sucked into the painting. My shift came quickly as I was lost in a sea of color.

"Hagan!" Panic ripped through my feathered body. I cried out again, "Hagan can you hear me?" My voice echoed. The path ahead changed from a colorful swirl to a black hole. A second before I flew through to the unknown, I found a gray crow confidently flying by my side. He took to his shift quickly, flying without any hesitation.

Dipping into the darkness, Hagan whispered, "Gray crow. Another piece of my mystery!"

A void opened into a cool night sky. The intuition of our new forms took us effortlessly to a location unknown to us in our conscious state. The clouds parted, exposing the dark sky and revealing a familiar scene below. It took the moment from surreal to frightening.

Landing on the branch of an all-too-familiar oak, we witnessed a group of horse-drawn carriages making a hasty exit. Scanning the scene, my corvid eyes were drawn to the butchering rock. Fresh blood was still dripping onto the ground. Far in the distance, in the open field, a gray wolf howled a lonesome cry. The sound reverberated so far into our surroundings the horses began to startle. I knew this was my moment.

"Chambers, fly!"

Like two war planes, we charged the caravan. We wove in and out of the frightened horses, causing chaos among the men. In an odd way, this unified attack felt natural, like he and I had played out this same scenario a dozen times. The butcher on his stallion turned to his team and commanded, "Ride hard and fast into town by the water's edge. A boat will meet you there. Stop for no one. We must see this mission through. Scatter men, scatter!"

The carriages continued onward while the single riders darted into the thick forest. Hagan made his move, eyes fixed on the butcher. He attacked his face, causing the horse to rear up in objection to the possibility of being subdued by this feathered warrior. A package fell off the butcher's waist to the ground.

"Mercy!"

Hagan didn't have to finish his thought transmission. I swooped to retrieve the package when suddenly the gray wolf ran in, beating me to it. The butcher regained control of his steed and retreated. I flew into the woods with Hagan following closely. The smell of lavender and eucalyptus drew us deeper into the trail. Hagan spotted two figures ahead.

Like seasoned soldiers, we stuck to the perimeter, quietly observing the scene. A man and woman were having a heated exchange. Suddenly the man came into focus.

"Hagan, that's Ash Sullivan!"

"What's he doing here? Who is the woman, Mercy?"

I couldn't tell from where we were perched. "We have to get closer."

Hagan flew to a tree not far from the couple, then noted, "She has the butcher's package."

The caw of his communication attracted the attention of our prey. As they turned their gaze toward the tree, seeing her face clearly sent me straight into the pain of my past. The world started to fade. I came back to my awareness, flying in the kaleidoscope. Hagan was leading the way when the black void dropped us back to the highest branch of my hanging tree.

A different air surrounded this place. The rock was no longer covered in blood, instead surrounded by the growth of nature's healing plants. Bloodshed had turned this ground into a sacred bed of comfrey, horsetail, and mullein. Hagan was fixed on what was happening below, and then I, too, was consumed by witnessing yet another gruesome scene.

Sensing his questions, I explained, "What you see below you is the body of Liam Anders. My executioner."

The good priest had hung himself from the very tree that had stolen my last breath. I would have been lying if I didn't admit to a feeling of satisfaction.

"Let's get out of here, Mercy." Hagan prepared to take flight when movement in the distance stopped us both cold. "Don't make a sound. Stay as still as possible. Slow your breath." As he uttered those words, I saw a young girl on the other side of the tree.

She had been standing unnoticed the entire time. There was no emotion on her face as she stared at the lifeless corpse hanging above her. Her eyes were hollow. I began to feel all my emotions move to my throat. As my wings began to tremble, I accepted the heartache of what I knew when I first laid eyes on her.

Hagan immediately connected his mind to mine, silently pleading, "Stay still, Mercy. Everything in me tells me we need to remain unseen."

As my mind prepared its telepathic response, the cause of noise in the distance was exposed. Out of the bush stepped Ash. In his hand, he held a solid black box with an X etched in gold surrounded by two crescent moons. He dropped to his knees and pulled the girl close to his body. I wanted to move closer, but Hagan was right. We needed to remain still and observe.

He gave her the box and started to speak. "Child, this box holds power from your origins. It will keep you, and those born unto you, safe. It is sealed by a magic key fashioned by the great makers of sacred things in the Carpathian Forest. Never open it. You will take this box to America, where you will start a new life. Do not linger here. It's time for you to move on, and discreetly. Little one, don't be frightened." He hugged her, slipping a piece of paper in her hand, and then disappeared into the bush.

I flew down and perched at her feet. In her hand was a boarding pass for the next ship sailing for America. I stared at her for as long as I could, memorizing every line in her precious face. Her dark brown hair was blowing slightly in a gentle breeze.

She looked down at me with her gray eyes and said, "Mother?" She reached her hand toward me, and Hagan suddenly flew between us. Startled, she turned and ran away, holding the box tightly to her chest, crying.

"How could you?" I screamed.

"We have lingered too long in a time that doesn't belong to us anymore. I don't know what's going on, but my mind isn't clouded with emotion like yours. We don't belong here, Mercy. We must leave." He flew away. "Mercy, now!"

The tunnel opened, and within seconds we stumbled through the painting, falling to the floor. The clock struck two o'clock as my mind continued to spiral.

Hagan held his hand over my mouth. "Stop screaming, Mercy." He held me close. "You've got to stop screaming. You're going to wake the neighborhood. Now isn't the time to fall apart."

"My daughter! My precious girl!" I was drowning in tears.

After a few minutes of self-soothing, I was ready to share what I observed. "Hagan, the woman in the woods with Ash was a woman in my vision. She was present before my execution. She's a witch. She gave me tea laced with my own medicine to render me unconscious so they could take me and tie me to the tree."

We lay side by side on the floor, staring at the ceiling. Hagan put my hand over his heart. "Mercy, there's a hard truth you need to stay in front of. The past is done. You witnessing these events shows the true marvelous nature of magic, an opportunity to see the spiritual thread you've woven through multiple lifetimes. Average humans would never get past the reminder of past pains. The sacred being in you knows this is all for guidance. Feel the pain, but don't let it cripple you. Store what you've learned in your arsenal of truth, for from that space of wholeness you will rise to be the magnificent giant this Universe has always known you to be."

He disappeared for a moment while I prepared a strong ginger green tea. Soon I would be leaving to embark on a new chapter of this unfolding. Suddenly, the sweetest sound filled the air as his violin poured out a lovely story. I closed my eyes and let it take me. It was a familiar tune. He walked through the house, my heart beating more rapidly the closer he got, until we found ourselves staring into each other's eyes.

This moment showed me intimacy in ways physical experiences never had. Pulling his shirt, I began guiding him into the lawn hidden between the two houses. The melody ran through every system in my body, stirring a deep flame from the very fire that made me. He stood without words, full of curiosity, clutching his violin and bringing the sweet melody to a halt. The moon, not quite full, shined just enough light to reveal the intrigue in his eyes.

Venus, steady at the moon's side, offered another version of magic illumination in the landscape above. I was enchanted by the agreements being exchanged all around us and between us. I locked into a gaze that dared him to look away. My hips began swaying with the rhythm of the universe. Movement took complete control of me. Hagan began playing softly as I delicately, intentionally removed my clothing.

Lost in the surrender of the beauty of simply existing, I danced, pulling in every powerful energy that offered support to my cause. Naked. Nothing between myself and the gods and goddesses of night. Serpents slithered from far and wide, creating a circle around us. My body honored those sacred animals, executing undulating waves of rich movement, clinging to every note Hagan emitted. We were synchronized, becoming one not with one another but with the collective. We were vessels accepting the music of the entire Universe, the song of existence, allowing the story of all time to pour through our hearts like an endless stream of Divine understanding.

The music stopped. He slowly walked toward me, stopping at a comfortable distance, allowing his eyes to explore my exposure in the most reverent way. As the snakes returned to the safety of night, he extended his hand. "Ms. Stone, may I have this dance?"

I bowed, never taking my eyes off him. "You may."

Our silent dance consumed us, filling our hearts with gratitude for a familiarity we didn't completely understand. He looked at me and I at him in a way that elevated the highest parts of ourselves. It felt like the whole Universe was watching with joy the exchange taking place.

"Mercy, I need to go. It's important I keep my distance for now from this new world you're stepping into. As sure as you are of your own path, my intuition will deliver me the same certainty when it's time." He removed a necklace from his neck, then lovingly draped it around mine. "It's been with me longer than I can remember."

On the end of a long chain was a series of seven intertwined rings of various metals. "Hagan Chambers Hoon, you, sir, are a man of great character. You are the one detail that, if removed, would crumble my quest before it begins. Take care of the sisters for me."

He kissed my cheek and disappeared into the dark night.

Chapter 6

Carpathian Forest

Lightning illuminated the dark sky beyond my window. I walked outside and waited anxiously on the porch. My heart started racing as my face caught droplets of rain off the wind. It was three o'clock in the morning, and there was no sign of Ash or Esther. I heard a shuffling sound coming from the end of the driveway. Placing my backpack on the step, I walked beyond the porch to investigate.

"Esther? Ash?" I whispered toward the noise.

Again I sensed movement at the end of the dark drive. Accompanying the motion were snarls and low growls. Some sort of animal was lurking in the shadows. Through the haze of humidity and rain, I could see it moving slowly toward me. Two purple eyes glowing in the shadow turned their focus to me. Emerging from the darkness, the gray wolf from my past life began circling me. The rain picked up to a steady pace. I stood there, frozen and frightened. All at once she charged, snatching my backpack off the porch.

"Stop! What are you doing?" I ran as fast as I could. I was about to catch up when she darted behind a building.

I felt her enter my mind. "Don't shift until I tell you it's safe. You're being watched. When you shift, fly straight up and high! There's a boat waiting for us at the river behind Café du Monde'."

Thirty seconds into her run she gave me the cue: "Mercy, fly!"

I set my aim straight to the sky. Hidden in the haze, I flew hard and fast to the river. Clarity into my past motivated my speed. Flying through nature's rage forced me to summon every ounce of courage within. The rain poured harder, leaving me only a sliver of visibility. As I struggled to navigate the harsh winds, my breathing became labored.

Faint shadows of flickering lanterns below confirmed my arrival into the French Quarter. Angry ripples of muddy water were crashing into the rocky banks at the city's edge. A small boat, empty apart from my backpack, was tied to the shore. Perching on a streetlight, I spent a minute catching my breath while assessing the scene from above. Seeing not a single person, I flew behind the cafe, quickly returning out of my shift. I ran down the bank and jumped into the boat. Suddenly, a blue crow started removing the rope.

Just as my boat eased away from the bank, the wolf leaped in. "My name is Ara Greystone." Still in her shift, she wrapped her body tightly around mine.

Water slammed the boat back and forth, nearly toppling us over. My hands were gripping the sides so tightly my knuckles were absent of color. "Where are Esther and Ash?" I screamed through the raging storm.

Her purple eyes stared deep into my mind. "Mercy, focus on surviving for now."

The raging waves were at war with some unseen force. Frightened, I clung to Ara's thick fur, burrowing my face into her neck. Sheets of bright electric light crackled all around so brilliantly I felt their illumination find swift passage to my buried eyes, mashed tightly closed. My mind, once filled with mystery and chaos, was now empty of all thought. Adrenaline fueled every level of awareness, aiding my fear's slow transition to courage. Surrendering to this new confidence, I found steadiness in my body. Upon opening my eyes, I immediately witnessed the blue crow who released us to this fate valiantly navigating flight among the powerful wind gusts.

"Must we be so dramatic in our conjuring?" Ara said with a chuckle, directing her amusement towards the blue crow.

"The stronger the electrical current, the stronger the cloak. You did ask for a proper vanishing spell, yes? Some witches are never happy," she said, laughing. Her voice was small but mighty, a perfect fusion of sea captain-meets-pixie energy. "The dead zone in the Gulf has expanded, blocking any direct pathway. Hang on! It's time for the path less traveled!"

Thunder exploded as lightening raged all around. The blue crow flew so high she disappeared. Briefly, calm found its way to us. Out of nowhere, a lightning bolt ripped the sky apart. From the middle of the flash, the blue crow descended like a torpedo, hard and fast into the sea.

"She'll drown!" I stood up, frantically, looking for any sign of her. The water was eerily calm.

Ara snarled, exposing her sharp teeth. "Sit down and brace yourself!"

The water began a boil originating from a gold light shining deep within the muddy darkness. A wave from below began pushing the boat further out as the light rose to the surface. From behind the magnificent wave emerged the biggest creature I have ever seen, a beast covered in black-and-blue iridescent scales, eyes made of silver flames with wings twice the size of her body. The storm returned to its rage. Observing this powerful sea dragon's maneuvering of the winds, it was no question this was the same blue crow who had started our quest.

She spoke effortlessly through the noise, with a voice as big as the sky: "I'm going to guide you quickly from the river into the Gulf. Whatever you do, don't shift until my cue."

She dove under the boat, reappearing several feet ahead. Her surfacing forced a huge wave that reached for the sky, tipping the boat further away from this marvelous creature. There were spikes seemingly made of metal adorning the end of her tail. Those sharp points suddenly attached to our boat. With great haste, we moved far and fast from New Orleans, Louisiana.

I felt the shift in my body when we crossed from the river into the Gulf — two immensely powerful, yet distinct, forces of aqua nature. The result of this collide is a dead zone. Nothing lives for long in this space of limited oxygen. Thunder shook the ocean floor. Heavy rainfall pounded the Gulf, creating death waves in the cursed waters ahead.

Our massive sea guardian began pulling us away from the zone. The waters raged behind us. Just as I was catching a breath of relief, believing we were leaving all that intensity behind, she took a sharp right turn.

In the middle of reversing direction, she looked deep into our minds. A true master of the sea, she playfully cast a magical shanty: "When fear steals your breath, and darkness fills your sight, surrender to your shift, find safety in the flight of night." She took off like a bullet toward the dead zone. The waters began swirling, toppling inward into an abyss.

I screamed in fear, "Ara! We're heading straight for a whirlpool!"

She leaned her body into mine, bracing for what quickly approached. "Mercy, steady your nerves and remember what she said!"

Just short of the edge of this newly formed abyss, our guide ascended. Hovering above, this majestic being cast a large shadow over our fate at hand. Fear squeezed my heart as I suddenly realized Ara had disappeared. In its downward spiral, the deafening water cascading into nothingness stole every ounce of light left in me. When the light leaves, the essence of the room is still behind. In this space breathes consciousness. We are in observation of our shadow. But this liquid abyss, this was not a familiar darkness. Ara was gone. Was this all a trap? Cycling darkness consumed me, shattering the boat that brought me here. I released my last breath to a forced leap into the unknown.

The sound of falling water slipped further behind me. The shadowy fall felt endless and cold. This unique darkness was the blackout birthed from oblivion, the alchemy that transforms into the great becoming. I was no longer sitting in the room observing divinity as an extension. This darkness was the collective. Divine within divine. I AM the never-ending cosmos here, I realized. Confidence extinguished the death rattles in my heart. Euphoria pumped sweet air into my lungs, triggering the memory of my first shift in the cosmic tunnel.

"When fear steals your breath, and darkness fills your sight, surrender to your shift, find safety in the flight of night."

That's it!

Bursting through multiple lifetimes, my red corvid state victoriously emerged. Burning to ash any residual fear in the oldest corners of my soul, I flew deeper into the black in a state of complete trust. Warmth from the comfort of surrender intoxicated every cell in my form. Every scratch collected on the surface of my heart began drinking in this atmosphere. A light, pure as snow, appeared in the distance. Pulsing took over the atmosphere in this oceanic womb of air and shadow. Feeling the song of battle drums in my core, I flew into the great white unknown.

I breathed the earth's oxygen back into my lungs. My feathers dampened, soaring through the clouds. Varying shades of blue masked the hole I had fallen through in the sky. Vanishing into a dead zone of oceanic abyss earned me favor from the Divine, I supposed. I felt daytime in the Great Mother's loving arms. She received me like a blanket comforting an infant from its first conscious chill.

I was baptized in beams of light, heat from the sun restoring the life within. I wept at the offering of such a precious gift. I'd always known Nature is sacred, but never had I valued the divinity of the Sun like I did in this moment. Rolling peaks of mountainous forest split clouds lingering low beneath me. The area was thick with trees. Shades of emerald decorated nature's canvas for miles, cloaking the inner workings of a world underneath it all.

A stream parting the trees below revealed a spot for rest. Immediately upon landing I returned my shift and rested my body on a massive rock at the edge.

Running water neutralized my thoughts, leveling any emotion that tried to tip my balance. The aching and burning in my stomach was the only thing I could focus on. Suddenly, the sun that had been so uplifting became too much to bear. Sweat was pouring down my face.

A mild tremor in the ground silenced the birds speaking in the trees. Every jolt summoned droplets of water from the stream upward to the sky. Darkness charged upstream on the shoulders of the wind, blowing exhaustion into my bones. A shadow of cold settled in as a ghost stepped in front of the sun. My body was losing its ability to remain present. Exhaustion held my eyelids hostage.

As I faded in and out, I could see the tops of the trees. It appeared the very land itself was moving me somewhere. I could hear the loud boom of drums in the distance. In my haze, through the in-betweens of exhaustion, I muttered aloud, "Sounds like a preparation for battle."

To my surprise, a bold, booming voice responded, "Not a battle. An initiation."

The voice came from high above. I realized the land wasn't moving me. I was cradled on the shoulder of a giant. Adrenaline kicked in as I stood up to assess an exit strategy.

"Calm down, little witch. I mean you no harm." He continued moving with caution through the edge of the forest. "Those drum sounds belong to the Apollonian War Wolves." He stopped and put me down at the head of the trail.

"This short trail goes down the mountain a bit. At the end you will find a lake with a small island in the middle. Wade through the cold shallow water and sit between the two bushes on the island. There you will find your guide." He turned his enormous body, once again blocking the sun, and began to walk away. His body was a perfect replica of humans, but magnified.

I ran after him. His stride allowed distance to grow between us quickly. "Wait, sir! Hey, wait! I don't even know your name." Before my eyes, this massive being, as tall as the trees, began to shrink. Still seven feet high in his new form, he turned to me and said, "My name is Vincent Black. You mustn't keep them waiting. Go. Now!"

His commanding voice drew all the words from my mind. Unable to speak, I turned to follow the downward path. I wondered if "they" were Ash and Esther. "They" could also be Ara and the Blue Crow/Sea Dragon. Did sea dragons inhabit lakes? Exposed tree roots demanded I use extra caution in every step of my curious wandering into, once again, the unknown.

Sharp, fiery pains ravaged my insides as the trail came to an opening. The damp earth transitioned to rocky terrain for the remainder of the trek to the small lake hidden in the valley below. Close to the water's edge, I could see a tiny, grass-covered island with two bushes adorning its landscape. Blue water mesmerized me, recalling memories of my journey through the ocean's womb. Reluctantly, I stepped into the shallow, cold water. A chill ran through my body, knocking the edge off the ache and burn.

I took a seat between the bushes, trying not to focus on my exhaustion. Thunder rumbled from the bright, sunny sky above me. How strange, I thought. Not a cloud in the sky. My eyes began to close when — BOOM — thunder shook and a bolt of lightning split the sky. A blue blur, released, plunged into the deep lake.

Some creatures sure know how to make an entrance.

I didn't think this lake was large enough to hold a sea dragon. Just like before, the water began to boil. A gold light illuminated deep within as bubbles began to surface.

"For fuck's sake, not another cosmic womb!" I said aloud.

A naked woman walked out of the water and said, "Cosmic womb. Excellent observation!" Water dripped from her short, coppery hair onto her beautiful chestnut skin. She extended her hand. "My name is Nyx St. James."

I placed my hand into hers. "Emerson Buckley Stone, but you can call me Mercy."

"You can call me Mercy,'" she said, laughing. "The famous battle crow!"

"OK, so you know who I am. Please, can you tell *me* who we are?"

She looked upward, drawing air from the sky. A cloud descended before us. Lightening flashed, blinding me. The space cleared, revealing a very regal Nyx St. James in a white hooded cloak.

Her honey-colored eyes were as warm as her smile. "To answer your question, sort of. Let's get you some food and a place to rest. *We* will start putting the pieces together once your power is restored." She turned and started walking on the water, continuing into the woods.

Following suit, I raised my foot to delicately step on top of the water. Splash! Sinking ankle-deep, I mumbled, "It was worth a try."

The burning in my stomach was starting to become unbearable. Sensing my discomfort, Nyx replied, "Your metabolism is on overdrive because of exhaustion and lack of food. It took you longer to get here than you realize. We need to quickly restore you."

"We? My life seems to be one giant 'hurry up and wait' moment. Speaking of giants, what crow is Vincent? Would flying there be quicker?"

"You are a curious crow," she said with a laugh. "'We' is my mentor. No, it's not Vincent. He isn't a crow. Shifting would be the death of you, as you've exhausted your magic. Curiosity and questions are only depleting you further. Patience, old friend."

We made our way up the mountain to the top of the ridge. Directly across from us, there was another ridge separated from ours by a lush, beautiful valley below. In the middle of the valley, a magnificent river breathed life into the dirt, nurturing earth's beauty. Certain parts of the river were overflowing into the surrounding terrain, creating pools of solitude along the way. I followed Nyx's lead and stood quietly, waiting. Waiting for what, I wasn't sure.

All at once, a golden eagle landed. Nyx acknowledged the beautiful being with reverence. "Hello, Master."

Nyx took my hand. "Mercy, you are such a brave human. If I asked you to walk off this cliff, would you?"

I looked into her eyes long enough to see that this was a serious question. Then I crept toward the edge of the cliff, scanning all possible outcomes of such a drop. My concentration was broken by sound of her loving giggle.

"Exactly!" she said. "You are the cautious daredevil in this lifetime. Game for anything, and certainly likely to always follow through, but only once you've analyzed every possible scenario. Listen, I'm not judging you. That strategy is remnants of the life of battle your origins were born into. However, in your original form, you wouldn't think twice about this great leap. You would run confidently without any shred of doubt into the unknown. This is why you are here first."

She embraced me, holding my heart close to her own. "The first task is acceptance. You nailed that instantly when you first encountered Esther. Throughout all your reveals, you never doubted the mystery. You never doubted the call to rise to your truth. You began the second task, trust, when you got in that boat. This is where we continue that lesson."

Her words fed me enough truth to ignite the fire inside, and though it was but a wisp of ember, it was determined. I turned to walk away from all of it.

"Where are you going? You can't just leave!" Nyx's voice rose with concern. The golden eagle calmly observed the scene at hand. Just as Nyx began to execute another plea, I turned and ran as hard as I could toward the edge until the ground was no longer under my feet.

Instantly, my arms shifted to red feathered wings, leaving the rest of my form human. Nyx was immediately at my side, mirroring my state. "Feet down. You cannot fly like a bird in this state. Arms extended, head back, heart to the sky!" I carefully copied every command. The minute our wings expanded, it stopped our fall.

"Mercy, keep your wings out. It will keep you suspended in the air. Now, like you are raising your hands to praise the sky, point them up."

Casting them up, I began to levitate higher than the cliff. The golden eagle remained on the edge and, if I didn't know any better, seemed amused. Mirroring the blue wings in front of me, I dropped my wings to the side, suspending me once again in the air.

"Mercy, drop your arms to the side, pointing down, and close your eyes. Once the surface finds your feet, open them."

We floated down, and as promised, the ground found my feet. I opened my eyes, discovering the most beautiful space. An enclosed glass bridge suspended high above connected the ridges on either side of the valley. The golden eagle joined us, revealing his true form upon landing. He was a powerful man, with ebony skin like a silky river under a new moon at midnight framing almond-shaped eyes as deep as the universe. White hair alluded to his ancient age and wisdom.

"Come, traveler. We have much to exchange. Nyx will prepare your quarters. You'll take your rest here for the evening." He gave her a nod, cuing her exit. She flashed me a reassuring smile and made her way down the long corridor toward the cave entrance.

Round tables surrounded by mismatched ornate chairs were scattered all throughout the walkway. He led me to a small table off to the side overlooking the river. I looked at the food on the table and was surprised by a familiar smell of home. "How?" I asked, knowing I needed not ask more. .

"Your grandmother is an Empress. I arranged to have her and that sister of hers..." Pausing, he raised his eyebrows, as anyone would after meeting Maxine. "...make your favorite foods. Please, eat. Restore."

Fresh bread, eggs, and cooked apples were a few of the many comforts of home spread out before me. "I feel like I haven't eaten in days." I ate a bite of homemade bread, closing my eyes, picturing Mim's kitchen. Warmth walked up my soul, tingling every strand of hair on my head.

Interrupting my nostalgia, the golden eagle spoke. "I am Solomon. It took you a day and a half to get here. That's the source of your discomfort. Shifting isn't something you do without consequence. One must navigate recreation magic carefully."

"A day and a half? It felt like minutes!"

"Portal casting is trickier the further it needs to take you. Had you the conscious ability to cast your own, you would have arrived sooner." He took a sip of tea and continued. "Portals are hidden wombs in the cosmos. Nyx has a particular gift for creating complex passages in the deep waters. Each element's portal is rooted in different intention. The womb creates space to ponder all of life's possibilities, and you, and you alone, have the choice to emerge or wander." He stared at me, deep in contemplation. "You are so cautious in this lifetime."

I looked out to the surrounding mountains, taking in a breath of grounding comfort. My body was satisfied, full of strengths of home. The sun hung lower, giving favor to the beginning of evening twilight, such majesty in nature's perfect landscape. I cast my gaze down to the river, now covered in the shade of early evening. "Tell me, Solomon. What have you come to say?"

Caught off guard, his hardened face softened into curiosity. "What have I come to say? I see your renewal has reached your wisdom. Walk with me, child of old. Let's take this down to the river."

He led me to a balcony outside of the enclosure. "I'll meet you below."

Quickly shifting, he soared down to the valley. I stepped off the edge of the platform. Finding my wings easily, I floated until the ground met my feet. Solomon was crouched riverside, hovering his hand above the water. A staff made of black oak trimmed in brass and iron arose from the water. There was a hexagon leveled along the top of the staff etched in gold. All at once, a realization washed over me.

"Solomon? As in THE King Solomon!" Such a surprising revelation. "Wow! And how?" My world wasn't much for traditional religious seeking. I respected all faiths, but this threw me. "That emblem is your seal, isn't it?"

"Surprised, battle crow?" He laughed, clearly carrying a better understanding of what was at hand. "Complexity through human evolution stems from the very spark that forms each soul. The origin of my flame held a sacred breath created by a perfect balance of earthly divinity. My father, a special king to the Earth God, was favored by many. My mother was a secret Priestess of an order of ancient wisdom — The All of All, an embodiment of Sacred Feminine.

"Mercy, in my time, women didn't have a platform to express wisdom publicly. History preferred preserving the political controllers of this world, the men. Kings and governments ran with focused efforts in power and fortune. The greedy would use their influence to achieve a status of respect and control. They had their religious tales of the One God, Only God, True God laying the foundation for their righteous bullying. However, the fear of losing those attributes hollowed the spirit of their mission.

"The women of my natural era honored the meaning of existence. As a vessel to creation, they held a link to eternity through their ability to nurture life. It gave them intuitive enlightenment to the sacred evolution of birth and death. Through cycles and seasons, they were assured life's promise of renewal and rebirth. It presented this ideal of ascension where one would strive to become aware and be better in every single incarnation, then one day transcend this world.

"Two layers of contrasting richness formed my need to explore all things evolution. I acquired an ability to understand the worlds of other beings. That path eventually led me to the deal I made for immortality. That deal happened on the day I met you." He turned to face me as the sun hung on to the last moments of day. "What have I come to say? Call your Master. Clarify your mess."

The authority in his tone stabbed a wound in my ego the size of a canyon. Defensively, I responded with anger, "Who's this Master you speak of? I know no Master!" A dark mist barreled through the valley on the end of my words.

Solomon raised his staff and blew his breath towards the dense shadow, forcing its retreat into the earth. "Calm yourself, warrior. Your ignorance is as powerful as your awareness. I watched you hang from that tree. Your fall to sleep is just as unstable as your waking up. One eye closed, one eye open. Energy is a power that creates magnificent chaos."

The dark mist revealed a flame of power inside of me. I walked closer to this wizard of immortality. "You speak in riddles, still providing no clarity to my query. Who is my master? Where did we meet, King?"

He thought carefully, then said, "The answer is one and the same. I encountered you during my ascension, after my death on earth. Your Master is the Great Keeper of Time, who you will find at the last doorway of Ultima Mortisto before entering the great beyond. Earth beings often refer to it as the veil. Red crow, you are the great warrior of that realm, the leader among the battle ghosts of the Universe. We made a deal, you and me. That deal changed the landscape of earth's spiritual mission so profoundly that it removed a chunk of memory of some of the most important beings of this time. I asked you for immortality. I didn't bargain for a deeper shadow over the great mystery I've spent my entire life trying to solve."

I couldn't tell if he was angry or afraid. Thousands of years old and no different from most basic human beings of earth. No amount of anger or fear can mask the desperation of need for selfish gain in any soul. Emerson Buckley Stone of Appalachia would loathe such self-serving motivations. But as I sat in observation through the eyes of my elevated Self, I understood instantly that he wasn't different from any other being in this Universe.

The opening chapter of nightfall had fallen upon us as stars reflected from the sky into the water. "Tell me the details of this deal, King."

Solomon began to point the seal of his staff to the ground, drawing a circle on the earth. In the circle's center, a stone emerged. He picked the stone up, hurling it high into the air. The wind began to rage, exposing a hole in the sky. A quick shift, and we flew straight up, blasting into the portal.

Solomon entered the chambers of my mind: "Trust is key. Allow your body to do what it's been programmed to do for centuries."

He flew so far and fast that I lost sight of him. My stomach began to burn as it had done after I first arrived. I could feel my shift trying to return. In the face of uncertainty, traditionally I chose fear, analysis of the situation, then surrender. Not this time. I flew harder and faster to the unknown. The burn pushed from my stomach into my heart, and then, suddenly, silver flames exploded through my shell.

I entered outer space as a silver flame. Such majesty in this expansive dominion of mystery and wonder. A shooting star launched past my trajectory. I screamed as my body continued changing. My sheer will forced this emerging form to follow the trail of stardust ahead. The flame of my existence morphed into a container. Inside, my body took on yet another form, while my essence remained the carrier flame of this mercurial womb. I was no longer the red crow, no longer a flame of the moon.

Strength radiated throughout my humanlike structure inside this soul vessel. Suddenly, a breastplate made of copper and covered in ancient symbols appeared over my chest. Rising higher and higher, I prepared for the next shift brewing. I screamed through the agony of the next phase of my evolution. I felt as if I were being burned alive as my powerful voice of pain bounced throughout the vessel.

An unbearable stinging in the palm of my hands and the center of my forehead revealed a permanent imprint, a symbol made of gold. The skin on my back ripped as my shoulder blades pushed themselves to the surface. The tears dripping down my face were blood. It was in this moment that, for the first time, I prayed for death.

The womb of my own essence continued supporting my trembling body, lifeless, in fetal position, as another phase began to unfold.

War was raging inside my being. The nauseating taste of metal overwhelmed every thought and feeling in my mind. My breathing began to slow. It felt like a wild animal was trying to claw its way out of my stomach. I suddenly felt the need to purge the contents of my mangled stomach. My face began to contort, forcing my mouth wide open, revealing a ruby-adorned pommel of a sword. Desperate for comfort, I pulled the sword from my body. Instantly relief, and, more importantly, determination flooded every cell of this version of myself.

I was utterly captivated. The red leather hilt transitioned seamlessly to a thick blade of meteoritic iron garnished in gold symbols. Fastened on my hips was a utility belt, also made of red leather, with an assortment of iron throwing stars in several pockets. Another phase began unraveling under involuntary war cries rolling from my lips.

A familiar burn crawled up my spine, making a path around my stomach. The sliver continued up my esophagus, forcing a cough that revealed a breath of fire. Under the element of fire, a snake made of quicksilver appeared. I gently guided her into my hands. As soon as her body touched the symbol in my palm, she began to wrap her body around the sword, spiraled toward the tip, and took her permanent place on the sword.

Raising my sword, I quickly ascended. Battle armor represented by a metal tin beak covered my face from below the eyes to my chin. The same symbols on my sword formed a line down the bridge of the metal beak. In my heart, I knew somewhere in my lifeline, this whole process was my truth.

Suddenly my vessel began to weaken in response to a distant, haunting sound. The walls of my carrier rippled with every hollow tone through the galaxy.

A choir of moaning ghosts summoned the final phase of my body. The burn, now a stinging, frosty cold, caused my exposed shoulder blades to shake. The silver vessel began to shift to a black liquid, becoming heavy. The symbols

on my battle gear and body illuminated space among the stars. The vessel burst into dark, forcing the final phase to reveal one last surprise. Wings of rose gold with red tips framed my body as I hovered above the outermost ring of Saturn.

I drew my sword and pointed the iron tip to the ground. A black shadow moved slowly toward me, like Jesus walking on the water. With a graceful stride that breathed no fear into my majesty, it spoke.

"The great sacred sanguine vessel. Saturn's red crow of justice. My greatest battle ghost of the final gate. Welcome home, moon child."

Chapter 7

The Veil

There's something to be said for the strange feeling of returning home when life, for such a long time, has had its way with you. It's even more grounding when the home you return to reminds you of the heaviness you previously survived. Perspective is a special magic on its own. I may not remember my life here, but I belong here.

A shooting star streaked by, quickly turning back, returning to the direction from which it came. The formless shadow spoke in weighted waves of nothingness. "He can't see us. He lost sight of you the minute you left Earth." Ancient comfort attached to eons of unknown wonders of the great beyond surrounded this voice of wisdom. I knew deep inside it was TRUTH.

"The Grand Authority of Secret Carpathia, Great King Solomon. He has spent many years walking the wrong direction to cross the in-betweens of the veil. No matter. Come, let's reflect inward on the focus celestial ground. We must move through the atmosphere in shadow. I'll shift you, but it's up to you to further the process. Let's see how you do."

Slipping off the ring, I felt my shadow fall into a sleepy mist following this master of obscurity to the planet below. Weightless, like a leaf on the wind, we drifted through the cold atmosphere. Static and roaring echoes in eerie tones rolled like waves through the space we traversed. Droplets of mist woven through my shadow began to harden. As we descended closer to land, the droplets scattered my form into a shower of diamonds.

As my feet captured ground, I became whole. What lay before me absolutely touched the flame within. The sky was a shade of dusky blue, holding a moon so large it looked as if it would crash into the planet at any moment. Its bright glow cast creamy orange waves across the navy sky. Off to the left, in the far distance, I had a moment of completion. My eyes held a sight so sacred. The end of me was staring into my beginning.

I was so moved. Tears once made of blood were now flowing silver and cold down my face. The arc of the rings, like a space rainbow of colors, flowed silver to amethyst to gold to jade and finally pooled into a soft melt of teal. The landscape was electric warm with soft rose lightning bolts scattering the mystery above. My marveling was suddenly interrupted by cautious movement behind me.

"The Moon is your home. You may not remember, but your essence knows."

I turned to witness a ghost solidify to a form cloaked in maroon robes, face hidden. Hovering above the head was a crown, a thin plate the shape of a hexagon made of lead and obsidian. "The great sanguine vessel of humanity. It's been quite the journey, my little warrior.

"I am the great End. The final gate. The Protector of Beyond as well as the protector of humanity. One cannot handle the other without the right alignment within. The vibrational chaos of a meeting of wrong timing between the two would unsettle the flow of the Universe."

"Aren't you just interrupting the natural order preventing such an encounter?" The ease of speaking to this Master of Finality had me forgetting everything that brought me here.

Amused, the Master replied, "I see we are picking up where we left off. Of course, you couldn't remember that this was also the last conversation you and I had. Your asking of it has me wary that this odyssey has all been for naught. When your unraveling reaches completion, my hope is you will understand the need, in even the most Divine, to maintain peace into the great beyond. Evolution never stops." The energy between us shifted from grounding to nostalgic. "I missed the silver flame in your eye."

There was a parental affection in the ghostly tone. "Did you create me?"

"Your origin? This is what you ask of me now? What is the moon to you in your current lifetime on Earth?"

"I am a Blood Moon Witch of Earth. The history I know speaks of 13 moons in a cycle year of Earth. Each moon birthed a divine being, a representative to that moon's intention. Those moons created the different clans of cosmic witches. As Blood Moon Witches, we represent Death among the living on Earth. Things end, and new beginnings must continue. The cycle infinitely repeats. In my current awareness, I understand I'm more than the present lifetime that holds me. But with so many twists and turns, the warrior in me knows uncertainty and confusion breed vulnerability." I felt a sense of urgency in this moment of truth-seeking, as if suddenly the blinders were removed. An awareness of enemies trying to manipulate my fate flooded my mind.

"Origins. Isn't it fascinating how even the most sacred truths are watered down over time? The message twists into a likeness of its first meaning. You are a creation of the great love of Saturn's moon Titan and Earth's moon Selene. That love makes you a unique witch.

"They exchanged philosophy of the beauty of shadow, the transformation of that work and the denial humanity places on its importance. Selene is a champion of Earth and the layers of power existing within that world. Her presence regulates the rhythm of Earth, guiding the cycles of life in that world. Titan is a keeper of the final gate of passage for humanity, the great battle ghost defender of cosmic preservation."

A hollow force of sound in the distance captured my attention. A luminescent, metallic blur was making its way toward us. "What about Hagan, Nyx, Esther, and Ash? Are they crow children of the moon, too?"

"Crow children?" The voice paused, thoughtfully. "Come, child, let's take this inside. The atmospheric wind is absorbed in thievish notions. They come curious off the trim of the veil."

A large boulder to the left suddenly revealed doors leading underground. We moved toward the entrance as they slowly opened, immediately releasing heat from below. As soon as we crossed the threshold, SLAM! I turned around to see that the door had vanished. There I stood in the middle of the most glorious temple with no doors, alone.

Dark, navy, wet sand flooring sparkled from the light of the lead-encased torches on the wall as the silver blue flames undulated upward. A stream of iridescent water snaked through the room, spilling under a wall to an unknown source deeper in the cavern. Heavy pressure weighted the air all throughout this massive space. The head of the stream came from underground, emerging from the feet of a sacred altar. A sculpture of a form rising in weary surrender was suspended mysteriously in the air, casting a shadow onto a diamond wall surface in the shape of a hexagon. Bright beams of rose-colored light poured through the diamond shell from the other side.

"The Last Gate," I whispered. I turned to greet the ancient voice again, but to my surprise, a Black Jaguar stood a few feet away, a beautiful beast with shadowed spot patterns framing fierce eyes that held dancing silver flames. "The other side of All is beyond that wall. You arrived at this system of life many ages ago from the other side. Your form that originally carried you into this space so long ago was that of a young child. I immediately saw the endless wisdom hidden behind that vulnerable shift. You entered my mind speaking only this: 'I am Grand Mor, the great end. It is my time to be here now.'

"You presented to be about six years old. However, you exuded ageless knowing. Stories of your existence were frightful among Divine Beings in this realm and beyond the veil. A legendary awareness from both sides attached a mystery of you belonging from another dimension all together. Beyond? What is beyond the great beyond? Your response to that question was always a fierce glance, a look that screamed finality.

"Titan is a moon of my gate and leader among the keepers of the realm. He and Selene, Earth's moon, consumed by love and parental notions, took you in. Although you came with a high level of understanding, you were far removed from how others experienced their role in this collective. Like true parents, they taught you everything they knew. Titan trained you in battle, although from my perspective, you trained him. Selene whispered her wisdom through every breath of your life with her. She illuminated the importance of exchange and growth in shadow. As all of you existed in the dynamic of immediate family, your own energy began to shift towards compassion for the human experience. It was then I knew you were on your own mission.

No matter how bold the Divine force, change is change and will always be the inevitable need calling from within.

"As time went on, Selene had children with a few different Divine beings. Titan, forever her true love, was often away fulfilling his role in maintaining the balance. Those children are the ones who became your siblings, not by blood but by bond. Your father spent most of his time with you keeping the gate, or sometimes in war with trespassers from beyond. Your mother tasked the rest of her children to be keepers of humanity on Earth and rhythms throughout the rest of the planetary system. These moon children are reigning over our galaxy creating their own lineage in the universe; hence the legend of the 13 clans. Even the ancient ones evolve.

"You and your siblings became the battle crows of Carpathia. Because of who you really are, you gave them the gift of shift. Each has a crow form, and each has a secondary form more specific to his or her other gifts. Some chose to roam the Earth living among the people, and some gave their offerings from a distance. You carried the blood of All through you so naturally you created the path of Blood Moon witchcraft, also called Essence magic. It was this love that opened the gate to your willingness to accept the deal that created this mystery that took the memories of so many."

The sacred jaguar continued explaining to me the many legends of my existence. When he was referencing the many different names associated with my identity, a strange noise silenced him. The roar of the atmospheric winds was now rushing closer to where we stood. Penetrating the smooth rock wall of the temple, a passenger blew in with icy wind. I grabbed a throwing star made of iron from my belt and threw it through its throat. The form vanished in thin air as the star returned on its own to my utility belt.

"Well done," the ancient jaguar said, nudging me toward the stream. "Human souls must endure an unraveling in order to continue their evolution on the other side of the veil. Most don't make it. Some cheat the system of evolution with second-rate magic. The people who obsess on their need to know ALL miss the biggest lesson of all. The Gate Breakers.

"'Knowing' is a product of existing in dynamics created in exposing yourself to as many differences to your own truth as possible. We must engage life around us. These experiences strengthen the cosmic thread within. So much of life's evolutionary process is the action of showing up. The result of this participation is a confirmation on how unique and important every contribution to that exchange is.

"The final gate is the reward for doing the work of the soul. The next elevation starts the process in furthering their divine evolution. Your instincts are sharp as ever. I see there is still no place for hesitation in your judgment and execution. Your iron sharps, blade and stars, are forged in the sacred fires of Mars. The symbols kissed in gold imprinted on your weapons and armor are charms from the universe, each providing an enhancement to your natural instincts."

I removed my sword from its sheath, admiring the artisanship. "What happens to the souls I kill?"

"No Death. You of all Beings should know there is no true end. Humans are given numerous lifetimes to achieve elevation beyond the veil. They play various roles, all to understand the beauty of willful exchange and surrender to the journey's endless possibilities. You did not kill the trespasser. You breathed new life into their chest. They lost all the lifetimes already invested, all the lessons successfully completed. They gained a clean slate and opportunity to start from the very beginning."

Splash!

The majestic creature jumped into the stream and swam under the wall. I followed, only to find, when the water met my ears, lonesome soothing tones of harmony enchanted my focus. The haunting tones were like the sounds of the atmosphere of this very planet. In the underwater tunnel, the floor began to rise until the surface met my belly. Bliss carried me into a swift euphoria. The surface was a whale lovingly pressing her body to mine. We exchanged wisdom. I gave through our brief touch my history and, in return, received the same. I suddenly found myself on the other side in a cave. The ancient form shifted back to the hidden figure behind the robes.

"You had a bit of a delay, I see." Amusement once again tinged the voice. "We are no longer on Saturn. Follow the cave out toward the light, and you'll return home, Mercy. I love that name. It's so fitting. Solomon will return shortly after you do. Time is different here. He opened a portal hitching a ride on a shooting star with no awareness of whether you even made it. You made a deal with him at the gate that somehow granted him immortality and turned you human. That deal remains a mystery to all. Best of luck, old friend."

I respectfully nodded, then made my way upward to the path's opening, stumbling upon a cliff. A voice whispered, "Surroundings are only clues. The flame of truth is inside of you. Go your own way." I jumped, and within seconds I stood in the valley back in the forest. Before I had the time to collect myself, a shooting star trailed across the sky. Solomon was very confused upon his return.

"As soon as I broke through this atmosphere, I lost sight of you. Where did you go, battle crow? Home?" I could not tell if he was genuinely curious or merely annoyed.

"I learned the minute we left that I have quite a bit more to learn, that's all." My tone was calm. One thing being a woman on Earth taught me was to be tactful in my wisdom in the presence of high-ranking masculinity until the moment is clear.

"I see. Well, clearly, you went somewhere. Any closer to finding a cure for this mess you made?" His voice projected authority.

"Mess I made? You mean the one we both made, Conjurer of Earth." My words came out stern.

Stunned, he paused and then replied, "Conjurer of Earth? I see you have been home. I'll need you to tell me everything so that we may resolve this uncertain fog in the minds of many."

"We?" I laughed. "Thank you for offering a space to rest my head. I'll be gone by dawn's first light."

He began to pace and look to the ground as if his next move would manifest in script in the very dirt between us. Panic in the most human corners of his soul journeyed toward my intuition. Humans, without fail, access their survival imprint when fear finds confusion. "Outcomes are fluid, conjurer. I'll come back for you when it's time. Until then, stay out of my way."

I shifted, flying straight up to the sky bridge above. Nyx, now accompanied by Vincent, was waiting to take me to my temporary space of rest. Seeing them together made clear an important change within me. I was beginning to settle into my truth, but the connection of the two lovebirds pained my heart with human memories of Abel and Hagan. I was now harnessing a vibration I didn't arrive with, showing me a bittersweet distance that was certain to grow between myself and humanity.

"You'll be resting in my favorite room for the remainder of your stay with us. Vincent insisted ground entrance would be more appropriate after your dramatic arrival into the Carpathian Realm. The earth can continue restoring your energy." She held him close, barely taking her eyes off him as she spoke. There was no question that she had not one care regarding any missing history, for she was living boldly for the present.

"Oh, Solomon is back!" Her tone was wrapped in full parental admiration.

I turned to see the conjurer standing at the end of the hall. His concern was hidden from those not looking but loomed large in my divine vision. "I'll catch up with you both in a minute. In the meantime, Vincent, would you mind showing Mercy her temporary home?"

Vincent smiled agreeably. Nyx hugged him then ran after her Master. She reminded me of LJ, with her voice and joy that were both larger than her physical presence. Vincent moved toward a spiral staircase. As I followed, I realized my intuitive connection had deepened since leaving Saturn. A layer of despair emanated off the back of this dove-like giant.

In a moment of compassion, I laid my hand gently on his back. "I sense you are troubled, Mr. Black."

He smiled kindly yet said nothing as he continued down the never-ending staircase. I removed my hand but again reached for his sorrow. "Whatever has filled you with dread, may you find peace in knowing that the guiding forces of nature are awake." I am not sure what prompted that statement, but this reuniting of my own new world/old world intuitive duality allowed an easy delivery of what needed to be said.

Vincent stopped halfway down the staircase. I found it odd, as we couldn't be much more than halfway down. Just as I was about to comment, the smell of vetiver, sweet tobacco, and ginger surrounded us: Ash's calling card. A golden door with a handle of obsidian manifested in the rock wall.

"This is where we must part ways, Miss." Seven feet tall, with a face full of divinity, he held both my hands. "Nyx is the greatest love I've ever known. The trouble you sense is my defiance. Solomon wants to hold you in a secret chamber underground. It is there he wishes to conduct magical experiments to, as he calls it, restore nature's balance. My father may have been an angel, but my mother was a magnificent priestess. If I know anything about restoring order to nature, I know that force isn't the way. Mother always taught me there's a fine line between actively drawing from natural resources and patiently meeting things at their natural unfolding."

There was a heavy layer of trust on every word he delivered. A purity in his eyes foretold a silent promise to do what was right. As I reached to open the door, he stopped me, leaving one final piece of wisdom in my ear. "Nyx is a warrior supporting a Master who taught her everything she knows in this current life, a Master who taught her a magic she never knew existed. However misguided you think her support may be, she comes from a space of passion for wanting to know the same thing you want to know: her truth.

Remember your name and my kindness when she expresses her passion regarding your absence."

He possessed wisdom without ego. I hugged him and, in that instant, felt a light burst through my chest. He was a special being full of purity. "Why are you helping me, Vincent? Why risk upsetting true love and a Conjurer who can possibly turn you into stone?"

He thought for a moment, then smiled. "I am helping you because it's the right thing for me to do. I felt the presence of my mother after you fell from the sky. Her magic was enough to convince me that I am to do whatever it takes to support your mission. True love prevails. Nyx has a passion as big as the ocean but sometimes can't see the forest for the trees. My trespasses will hopefully spark her own desire for independence."

Slowly Vincent opened the door, revealing a hallway of nothingness. He turned to me and said, "As for the Conjurer, this necklace shields me from being controlled by magic." It was the same necklace Hagan had given me — seven rings of varying metals intertwined. "We've spoken too long. You must go. Quickly!"

The moment I stepped into the dark, the world behind me disappeared. I sensed movement in the void but couldn't see anything. I followed the vetiver, knowing it was leading me to Ash. The fragrance was so bold it took me back to the first moment I met him in Mim's house, the beginning of my grand fool's journey. That day not only felt like a lifetime ago, but it also felt further from my inner knowing. My thoughts were suddenly broken by a familiar sound.

"Ring-ring."

The haunting sound of a telephone ringing was the only other presence on this dark path. I kept moving forward although my eyes saw nothing.

"Ring-ring."

The sound grew louder and louder until finally a telephone appeared at what seemed to be the end of my path. I felt someone breathing on my neck in the dark.

"Ring-ring."

The next breath I felt slipped off the edge of a whisper, "Well? You going to answer?"

CHAPTER 8

Goddess of Another Time

"Hello?"

"Ms. Stone, Dr. Sullivan will see you now in the library for a nightcap." Click. With the soft, feminine voice on the other end came an awareness that I was now standing in entirely foreign surroundings.

Every square inch of the large luxurious room dripped with elegance. A crisp breeze blew softly through an acorn-framed, open stained-glass window. The opening revealed an exposed night sky hovering above what appeared to be an endless castle. My senses began to scan the chamber. What they perceived was a column of shelves holding ancient books from the floor to ceiling and crackling noises from a small fireplace that breathed healing promises of sanctuary. A new feeling washed over me. My blood was warm. My heart started to race, when suddenly... "Ring-ring."

"Ring-ring."

"Hello?"

"Ms. Stone, Dr. Sullivan is waiting for you. Do you require some assistance, or will you be heading this way immediately?" This time her tone, although pleasant, was a bit sharper in delivery.

"I'll be right down!" I answered, my own wicked tongue returning the energy.

I opened the door to a private stairwell. The casual spiraling descent revealed horrifically beautiful dark art at every turn. I found myself aroused at the nature of what each piece expressed: images of death, war, birth, sensuality, accomplishment, and the unknown displayed in the darkest ways. The last step led me to a wall, a dead end displaying a large painting of a woman. She had hair as black as night with skin made of gold. Two fingers of her right hand were raised to the sky. Two fingers of the left pointed below. The great balance of both worlds. Her hollow eyes cried a never-ending stream of iridescent tears.

Suddenly, I realized there was no door. How do I get out of here? I touched the stream of tears on the painting, uncovering a memory. Flashes of a life here ran through my mind's eye. Almost all the images were filled with laughter or primal screams of passionate release. Intuitively I whispered, "As above, so below," and walked immediately through the painting, entering a common area at the end of another hallway.

A smooth cobblestone hallway led to an inner courtyard in the castle. Lanterns illuminated the open area, which smelled of cooked apples. The warm glow under a starry sky created a relaxing ambiance. He stood there, staring into space. Deep in reflection, his presence projected a cool breeze. The source of his burden clawed its way up my spine, sending a chill all the way to the very tips of my hair. Its cold clutch gripped my heart, forcing each beat to steady with purposeful contraction.

Thump-thump. Thump-thump.

The quivering in my body extinguished my inner fire. A steady footing anchored me to the ground.

"Cold?"

Turning to face me, his voice met my ears at the same moment our eyes engaged.

"Comfortable." My reply slipped through my lips off the edge of a voice that was me but layered in rich divinity.

Lines on his face, once sharp, suddenly softened as he received the fullness of my voice. Taking full advantage of his silence, I took the floor: "I am more myself than I've ever been. Yet, I still don't know who you are, Ash Sullivan, professor of divination studies, love interest of the Queen of the Eastern Realm of Saturn, watcher over my path. Enlighten me."

He laughed, handing me a warm mug. "Your favorite." Steam drifted from the cup, delivering fragrant nostalgia in cinnamon-apple flavoring and rum. "I picked them earlier from your favorite spot in the orchard while you were making the quick trip home. Well, one of your homes."

I stood speechless, holding the warm mug with both hands. Slowly, he took one step toward me. I heard faint echoes of bliss in layers of heavy atmospheric tones within that small space between us. His bright eyes were captivating, and deep under their surface flickered a light as bright as Venus.

"You and I have known each other for quite some time, Mor, Keeper of Death, Guardian of Humanity and the Great Veil, War Crow of Fate."

Observing the shock of hearing him speak my identity, he raised my cup to my chin and instructed, "Breathe the steam deep into your womb. Let the moisture reach the source of your well. Absorb this fragrance of the cosmic soul, the giver of life. Breathe the sweetness of abundance and protection. In the pursuit of passion, sip this soothing potion. Allow its warmth to deepen the chill of our connection, aromatic magic uncovering knowledge of ancient realms."

I drank the cup empty of its magical contents. Ash followed suit. Electricity exploded inside my body. I had no words to offer him. In that moment, every emotion conceived throughout time swirled outside of me in spiraling fury. Yet, I remained quiet. I was lost in observation of what had become of my purpose.

"Let it take you. Its draw feeds on your desire." He stayed close.

We were two beings holding our sacred cups of mind-altering magic. In a moment of spectacular clarity, I had another unveiling. I presented my hand to him, palm up. Looking into the shadow of his eyes, I boldly proclaimed, "I stand in front of you with no conflict of intention."

Without pause, he tapped my palm three times with the forefinger of his left hand. A copper skeleton key emerged slowly from the center. A tickling sensation climbed up my body as he pulled the key from my being. The right corner of my lips twinged from the pleasure.

"We made our own type of hidden magic ages ago." He held the key to the sky. "Tonight we enter a space left cold by our absence for far too long. Tell me, Goddess, what is your heart's desire?"

"I desire to see, by sacred three, what's hidden from me!"

A gothic door slathered in red fell from the sky. He threw the key into its iron lock. I put my hand in his, and, slowly, we made our way through. Suddenly, the dark forest cradled us in another place altogether, a place layered in colors of fiery autumn in the night. The door vanished, revealing no more castle, only trees with crooked branches masking mysterious night noises. Draped in heavy emerald velvet cloaks, we stepped forward into the willing earth with clear intention.

Power charged in the ever-changing seasonal space between, emanating the purity of winter through the shadow pulling us deeper into the night. The air grew colder and colder. It grew so cold my body shook in never-ending rhythms. We came upon a clearing nestled by a lake that mirrored the night sky.

Ash stepped closer to my body. Sensing my quiver, he retreated, stepping back a comfortable distance. "I forget sometimes you aren't entirely you. This magic doesn't create space for you to surrender and release. I, and all I am, connecting to you, in all that you are, creates a magnificent fusion of divine power. This magic sees the highest parts of our being and the strengths each of us bring to the universe around us. There is no submission nor dominance in this ritual."

He walked to the only tree affected by this winter chill. Naked of its leaves, it stood out among its counterparts dressed in shades of red, orange, and gold. "Mor, do you know who I am?" Vapors lingered in the cool air off the force of his last word.

The information was in the front of my wisdom like words from the pages of a book, only the language was something I'd yet to remember. I stared into the sky, my eyes stopping on the brightest spot. A gust of wind blew through me, revealing his sacred identity.

Empowered by this revelation, I removed my cloak, revealing the flesh of my body for his eyes to worship. Snow began to fall from the heavens when I commanded, "Tell me, bearer of eastern light, Lord of Air, Lucifer Morning Star, what is your heart's desire?"

He grabbed my cloak, laying it on the ground. His black painted nails were filed to a dull point in the center. He traced the tip of one nail down my cheek, around my neck. Making his way down my sternum, he inserted the tip of his nail enough to draw a tiny bit of blood. Grabbing my wrist tightly, he proclaimed, "I desire to see how the world once knew me, by the light of Venus, to form a true reality."

He licked the tiny blood stream between my breasts with his icy tongue. His eyes shut in pleasure at the taste of divine life. He mumbled through desire, "Reinvention."

My body, still in transition, was yoked to a human component that couldn't quite master the adjustment to the cold. The winds of night blew snow hard into my exposure. I moved close to his body, nestling into his arms.

"Are you cold, Goddess?" He opened his cloak, pulling me into his covering, exposing the cool temperature of his bare flesh underneath. The contrast of warm fabric and his cold form sent a shiver through my body that visually rolled out off my shoulders in a shudder. "Skin holds an incredible amount of neurological intellect. Chills awaken pleasure cognition, stimulating awareness in your body."

He dropped to his knees in front of me, exposing my form again to this temporary moment of winter. Cold hands delicately clutched my hips. The shiver of the season shifted to a quake of longing. "Stay present, Goddess." He dug his claws gently into my skin.

I cast my gaze downward. Our eyes locked instantly, forcing a cold breath of salvation back into my surrendering lungs. His eyes grew black, leaving only a flame of magnificent light in the center. I held his face in my hands. "Angel of Night, your beauty is extraordinary." Staring into his light, euphoria swept through me. I felt my power start to rise.

"That's it, Goddess. Meet me where I am." He started to draw his claws down my body. Subtle traces of those sharp points slowly crept to my inner thigh. Scratches in my skin formed a pathway, marking his touch. Lingering at all the right moments, he continued softly carving into my flesh, dragging his sharp edges all the way to my feet. Faint lines of blood began to highlight the scratches, and I noticed a stinging sensation, a dramatic contrast to the chill in the air and his touch.

Snow fell all around, sticking to his long black hair. I ran my fingers through the loose locks, pulling his icy breath into the sting of my wounds. The freezing atmosphere made peace with my resistance, finding my bones settling into the comfort of quiet cold. He passed his cool tongue over sections of broken skin, healing these scratches with his soft affection.

I grabbed his hair, forcing him to stand. Breathing deep, his nostrils flared like a beast savoring the calm before the charge. I took his cold thumb into my mouth. Removing it, I guided the wet, sharp tip to his own cold chest, forcing a small puncture under his diaphragm. I leaned in...

He jumped. "Easy, love." Blood streamed down the center of his body. He threw his cloak to the ground and pulled my back into his chest, holding my breasts with his cold hands. Softly he kissed the top of my shoulder, sending goosebumps over every inch of my flesh. Leaning into my ear, he whispered, "Blood is the force of life. Tasting mine officially puts this ritual in motion. Sex divination requires powerful control. You will want to submit to me in the depth of your pleasure. You will want me to pull the heaviness out of you over and over so that you may cast your spells into the night. However, you mustn't go there. This ritual isn't centered on release."

He pinched my nipples as hard as he could, and I screamed in ecstasy, the echo like a banshee traveling through the void.

"Don't scream, Goddess. Let it build." Once again, he pinched them, this time driving in the tip of his nail, summoning a tiny speck of blood. I fought the urge to scream by pushing the energy deep into my body. The power began to grow inside of me, gifting me clarity. My deepest self assured me I had been here many times with him.

Confidently, I broke free of his hold, gaining control. Our cloaks crumpled on the ground, providing a makeshift sacred earth temple. I pushed him to the ground and climbed on top of his body, devouring the magic that made him.

"Stop. Mor, stop!"

From out of the ground, he summoned an ancient athame. I grabbed it without thought, drawing a small bit of blood from my left hand. He took the offering, tracing a six-pointed star on my chest. The mark of the morning star. Taking the athame, he drew his own life force. I took his taste offering, then began to draw a full moon surrounded by two crescents on his chest. The mark of the Goddess.

Snow fell heavier as our carnal ritual began to unfold on nature's altar. I found such pleasure pinning him down, exploring every inch of his cold body. Every intense moment in our slow rhythm brought us closer and closer to the animal force within. Just as we reached the edge of completion, he playfully tossed me off of him and ran to the water's edge.

He stepped into the water and held out his hand. "Earth through the blood of our passion holds our essence now. Come to me, Goddess."

Chilly water covered my feet as I entered the dark lake to join him. Kissing my third eye, he guided me further into the deep. As the water caressed my waist, I felt the presence of eyes. Turning my focus back to the shore, I spotted three black crows and a black fox standing quietly in calm power.

"That's a layer of our earthly forms, isn't it, Morning Star?" I had no sooner asked the question when my mind told me the answer. No more shaking. No more cold. He did not answer. Letting go of my hand, he disappeared underwater. Diving under, I instantly realized I was in Divine form. Normal human reasoning for existing in this space didn't apply to me. A light faintly shone in the darkness. I swam hard and fast, straight into his arms. I wrapped my legs around him, and we held each other. The energy we summoned on land required a shift in the deep water. Our connection commanded calm waters around this union. The pleasure was building from the intimacy of simply holding each other. His eyes hinted a threat of sacred orgasm. I denied his urge, bolting like a shark to the surface.

The cold air shocked life back into my wet body. My crows perched on my form as I looked deep into the eyes of the fox. "Come and get me!" I shouted. Steam began to rise from the water, announcing the arrival of my sacred lover. As he approached the shore, I walked backward, facing him slowly, lowering my cold back to the ground. The earth revealed a circle of embers, and I felt his power with every step he took.

He dropped to his knees two feet from me and crawled the rest of the way until he was on top of my body.

"Through the trials of our control, may we revisit our intention, origins."

I grabbed his throat and pulled his chest to mine. Loudly, I proclaimed, "To Restoration and Reveal!"

His body was no longer cold. The heat he possessed provided the right amount of pleasing discomfort. The earth gave us permission to engage. The water gave us comfort in our partnership. The flame of the fire pushed us beyond the edge. Pure ecstasy caused our physical forms to catch fire. The embers burned the shell away. It left us standing outside the flaming circle watching our shadows continue to have the most intense sex imaginable.

Time stopped around us, yet the dramaturgy within the circle never ceased. I grabbed his hand. "We really do complement each other in the realm of euphoric connection." Our shadows continued to twist and turn into each other like wild animals in the fire. The scene drifted farther from our sight, replaced by a voice speaking silent truths privately in our ears.

The ritual gifted me the divine message to my silent thought:

'Lucifer Morning Star is the shadow of humankind. The shadow of the very Earth. Part of your ascension ritual to evolve the Morrigan required you to visit the three divine aspects of yourself. His freedom is too bright for a young humanity. Therefore, their turned backs assign him the role as shadow. Tempter of comforts. Igniter of individual evolution. His anchoring in secret parts of their minds awards him a certain dominance over the power that lingers on Earth.

The perfect version of feminine divinity within his psyche is you. That invokes an automatic reverence for your power. He will never harm you. Your paths are similar in the world. You arrive as fate at the end of the journey accepting only the willing souls to ascend. You both recognize that freedom gifts a recognition of inner divinity to the ones brave enough to claim it. At the gates of fate, you give them the choice, knowing it will move them forward or backward depending on their clarity within the lessons. This very ritual started the event that twisted your fate so deeply you ended up here.

Your higher selves know you are retracing the events of that moment. The time to climax is close. Orgasm in sex magic awards liberation. Bold, detached liberation is the key to experiencing the other side of the cosmos. Let the night unfold organically, knowing you are repeating the same events of past efforts.'

My body began to burn and quake when suddenly we simultaneously were present in the act of primal salvation. As the ritual found its end, the season shifted back to autumn's natural grace. The red door appeared as we wrapped our weary bodies and returned to the castle.

In the courtyard, a table was decorated by marvelous foods. Ash pulled out a chair, offering me a seat. "Our partnership has existed in this space before

humanity reached the edges of this magical forest. Now we feast and replenish the energy purged."

There was no conversation to be had as we both hung onto our presence by a thread. The exchange between two divine beings. We shifted energy in the very atmosphere we occupied. A dead silence fell all around as the Earth also had to replenish the force we manipulated during our holy ritual. We both knew this was a once-in-several-lifetimes event on this planet. Aether, the fifth element, is the material that fills the universe beyond the bounds of Earth. The Earth wouldn't exist if we continued giving and taking aether at rapid rates.

"Thank you for being the friend I know you've been for so long. I'd like to spend a few days lying low here so that I may formulate my next execution. Would that be all right?"

"Stay as long as you like, Goddess."

I stood up to make my way back to my quarters and suddenly recalled my door painting. Stopping, I turned to Ash. "I meant to ask, who are the identities of the other two paintings close to my quarters?"

He thought carefully before replying, "That's for another time, Ms. Stone."

Bliss wasn't the word for the energy that carried me back to my room. It was satisfaction from lingering intoxication filtering through intense focus. The stairs up to my room, however, were daunting. It became clear to me that my body had reached its breaking point. Entering the room, I was comforted by the feeling of home, which prompted a lump in my throat.

Managing memories of Saturn, New Orleans, Abel and Hagan, and even more heartbreaking, Appalachia and Mim, flooded me with emotion.

I woke up on a luxuriously soft bed with rose-colored silk sheets. Running water called me from this comfort. Searching for the source, I found myself at the far end of the grand room. A few steps up led to a raised common area that poured out through two French doors to a balcony. Ash was out there, standing over the most delicate clawfoot obsidian tub trimmed in gold.

"You called out to me in your thoughts," he said, pulling me close.

"What happened? Was it all a dream?"

"You were exhausted from the extremes of the day. I found you lifeless in bed moments after I heard your call."

Confusion fogged my mind. I wasn't sure who I was or what was real. He began removing the robe I was wearing, exposing the scratches on my skin. A tingle traveled on the end of a memory, grounding reality back into my being. He traced his nail softly down my back, instructing me to get into the tub.

The water held the perfect temperature, flooding my body with relief. Iris petals were floating in the water, as the smell of damp, crisp earth lingered in the air. Sitting on a small stone to the side, he pulled my long, dark hair over the edge. "The irises grow year-round abundantly below your balcony as they've done for centuries. I still forget you aren't all you."

"You're wrong, Ash. I'm becoming more myself than even you know. I am human as well as holder of the space in between, protector of the Great End and Beyond. I may not understand the fullness of that place. I may not have complete clarity, but make no mistake, I am ALL ME. In every way." I slipped deeper into the water.

"Of course. However, for as long as you entertain the emotional ties to humanity, your vulnerability will stand in front of your divinity. You will always have to fight through a shadow to get to your power," he said, each word spoken with an aged ring.

"Isn't that what humans do every day? I'm learning a lot about my worth in this Universe by surviving that challenge. I may not remember specifics, but my experiences imprinted an understanding in my soul of the value of exchanges layered in love. How lucky the beings are who are intertwined in the human ascension project. Rich depth is at their very fingertips every day. Mystery and shadow birthing life towards something beyond what they already are. Shouldn't that work for all beings? Even if we must construct our own pathway?"

"I'm not sure if I'll ever understand you, Goddess, but I trust your process. I always have." He pulled delicately at the strands of my hair.

"Tell me the story of us, Morning Star. Would you?" I stared into the night sky.

"Us. This Earth was in its season to begin natural evolution toward its first intelligent species. Old magic breathed through the elements, gently guiding their unfolding awareness as it always has and will do. I had gotten quite bored with my own path. I tried another. I struck a partnership with a fellow God that literally went south, and there you were. The Grand End. The Mother of Fate.

"My blinding light slipped right past you, exposing my loneliness. You showed compassion to my shadow. You came in and out of my life on the winds for thousands of years. Entering always with a grand importance, you spoke divinity older than anything I had ever heard. You arrived often physically beaten from battles you never spoke one word of.

"This place, the Effect, was created as a sanctuary for powerful beings looking to recharge and study without philosophical or physical interference. The consequence of action/cause produces an effect. You taught me that within those exchanges are the hidden gems of life. The borders here are magically designed to remove energy that isn't agreeable. Your room can be occupied only by you. No matter the being, no one can enter that space or any space on the grounds that isn't designed for their own needs. The grounds and libraries are communal. This balcony is as far as I can go in your space here. I brought you here a few ages before you entered your Battle Crow of Justice era."

"A friendship that has survived the ages. Wait a minute. You heard me calling but can't come in? I woke up in bed, but I had just walked through the door. If you can't come in, who put me here?" I felt sleep pulling. "I know my family is worried sick over me. I should probably check in." This was the first time I had felt the weight of missing everyone from that life. Even Abel. The ebb and flow of my humanity was overwhelming.

Ash stood up, holding open a silk robe. "As far as how you made it to bed, well, that's yet another mystery that will remain. For now." He laughed as if he were holding the secrets of the universe. "Time to get out, Mercy. You need rest. Home can wait until the morning. Technically, you have been gone only three days. Solomon contacted your family on arrival. They know you are safe."

I stepped out of the warm water into the cool night air. "Speaking of Solomon, his intentions are less than favorable, and quite frankly, his tone irritates me altogether. I will address his attempt to keep me as soon as I recover my strength."

"Easy. He is a brilliant sorcerer and a bit of a madman. Solomon spent his natural life expanding his own magical knowledge. In all his wisdom, post-life, he somehow managed to convince you to aid his return to Earth upon meeting you at the final gate. Although it is selfish motivation, he knows deep down he's partially responsible for Vincent, the battle crows, and other beings in this realm losing their memory. In the form you are in now, you are no match for him. You have recovered Divine memories, but your body in this state is in pieces across the Earth.

"Research a bit during your stay. When the time is right, you will get back to your human life and honor the mission that brought you here. Find your missing pieces. The world sees you as Emerson Stone, Appalachian healer. The rest know you as the great battle crow of Saturn. I am the only one who knows who you really are, Goddess. Let's keep it that way. Look around your quarters for clues. I'll show you the library after brunch tomorrow so you may continue your research."

He shifted into dark fox form, leaping down to the bed of irises below. The smell of earth left in his absence soothed my weary senses. As I made my way back inside my quarters, the chill of night had me yearning for warm comfort. The room had so many areas to explore, but the warmth from the fire insisted my focus start there. The interior of the room, a Gothic Baroque grandeur, was so boldly detailed it would paint blush on the hollowest of ghostly faces. It was a room that breathed its experiences through its walls. The magnificent room was bathed in a soft glow from a line of black chandeliers mounted from the main entrance to the balcony.

Hand-carved furnishings were scattered throughout the large space, and I was drawn to a desk in the far corner of the room. Considering the proximity of the books, it would seem this was my study area. I sat behind the desk, immediately exploring the pages scattered over the surface. To my left, the fire spoke its primal language with every whip of the flames. A book bound in red leather, *The Road to Iris,* lay open to page 27. It seemed to stare at me, pulling my focus to the last paragraph.

"The origin inside the shell breathes in three layers. Existing in the lowest realm, one finds oneself on the journey of humanity. Shining brightly in the highest realm, the origin reigns in pure divinity. Occupying the mid realm is fate's bridge. The sage sees wisdom in the ascension. The dreamer finds blind trust and will in the early stage. The Master finds steadiness in both. The Master adds texture to the future while finding earth in the past. The Master of the in-betweens stands on fate's bridge, blending the elements through their own existence. That's the alchemist's evolutionary magic."

The book continued to speak on the three layers until page 33 revealed a handwritten note:

When shadow covers thought, stand under the arching stream that pours from the iron chalice and cast your eyes down.

I must have been staring at the cryptic message for an hour when my body pleaded with me a final time to take my rest. I was so tired I couldn't sleep. Thoughts of Abel flooded my mind as the comfort of the bed began to cast its spell. I was reminiscing about the night we met. Growing up in small-town

Appalachia, I had limited exposure to the outside world. My trips to Aunt Maxine's throughout my late teen years made an impact on how I adapted to this world. The magic that city held reminded me, when I stepped foot into her world, of the magic buried in my humanity. That magic city reminded me of the divinity within.

One night, LJ and I were in a club on Bourbon Street, drinking and dancing so hard it elevated our light like a beacon in the sky. A hypnotic song started summoning movement in my body. My soul hovered just above the surface of my shell, calling in its own adventure with every pulse. I made my way to him where he stood, shrouded in mystery, in the corner. Dancing in front of him, I explored my body, guiding my hands in patterns of sensual traces. He wasn't amused at my forward approach and left the bar.

Later, over midnight coffee, LJ found a lover to engage for the rest of the evening. Our waitress couldn't resist her intoxicating charm. They made their way to who knows where to see what the rest of the night had to offer them. I walked down the empty street at 2 a.m. Street lanterns flickered in the calm darkness. I turned a corner and saw him standing under a streetlight.

"Hello," he said, with a curious smile. "I'm Abel Saturnali."

For the next two minutes we just stared at each other. I didn't respond to his greeting. Instead, I sized him up like a predator stalking a victim. Immediately following that silence, we started to kiss, and the next thing I knew it was morning, and my body was equally tired and sore from a night of intimate warfare.

I asked him, "Why did you leave the bar?"

He looked at me and said, "I saw my undoing in your eyes. In my career, I observe things so full of wonder they'll enchant the mind, in the most extreme way. Yet, you hold such magnificence, the sheer reach of it almost took every breath from my body. My instincts told me to run."

"And here you are!"

I still remember his smile when he replied, "And here I am."

A fog rolled through my mind, interrupting the memory of that fateful encounter with the man who would capture my human heart.

"Mercy! Mercy!"

My eyes flew open at the sound of Abel's voice in the distance. Jumping out of bed, I ran to the balcony.

"Mercy! Are you there?"

"Abel, is that you?"

"It's me, Mercy. Come to me!"

In an instant, I shifted to my red crow form and flew deep into the wood beyond my window.

CHAPTER 9

The Initiation

My bare feet landed on the mossy forest floor. Darkness surrounded me. As I stepped forward, I became aware that I couldn't see anything. My eyelids were frozen shut like the hinges on a rusted door. Although I couldn't see her, the moon was full, and I felt her illumination stimulating my skin, pulling me deeper into the forest. I walked slowly through ghostly air. Moisture from the fog washed over my eyes, allowing them to open.

The sight stunned me.

It was no longer night. Time had reversed, or perhaps sped forward, to the subtle light of early evening. In an instant, I realized I was barely connected to my senses. Am I dreaming? I wondered.

I continued to wander the forest. It was eerily silent. My vibration began to rise. I began feeling more present in my body. Settling into the void, I transitioned from confusion to peace, focusing on the surrounding reality. My hands were heavy, carrying something warm and wet.

"Mercy!"

The sound of Abel snapped my mind into full focus. I looked to the burden in my hand, only to find I was carrying a human heart. The delicate force was still warm, covered in fresh blood. A high-pitched frequency was ringing through the stillness, and all at once I became whole. My mouth brought me to life as my soul raged. I woke up in my awareness fully, screaming into the nothingness of that lovely autumn void.

My song wailed through the dying leaves, calling in winds of freedom and light. Cold chills ran up my legs, sending a shiver up to the exposed hole in my chest. I was a ghost, wandering heartless, screaming my shadow into the great wide nothing. Up ahead, the forest resumed its natural rhythm of dark night.

Heavy energy floated my hollow body through a clearing in the woods. The moon offered a ceremonial light that shined with intention on a lone ash tree in the distance. The darkness began to swim in waves in front of me. The sky and the ground melted together, then swiftly pulled apart.

Is this a dream?

A soft rain kissed my face. I became drunk, swimming through a euphoric disorientation. My sights tunneled into kaleidoscope patterns of amber, gold, and gray. Peace found the center of my soul and took me into the void.

Surrender.

Release.

I awoke into complete tranquility, but the world was upside down.

Somehow, I was hanging from the ash tree by my right leg.

A tree. The humor of it all.

A swarm of butterflies flew by with a swift whisper, taking the form of a shadow woman with obsidian eyes. She walked toward my hanging body and leaned into the hole in my chest. In a quiet, tonal whisper, she softly sang, "The original mission is to become whole." She breathed smoke into the emptiness of my wound.

"Heal the human. Heal the goddess. Maintain the bridge by taking the knowledge of who you are, and complete this mission."

The form dissolved, echoing, "The calm you feel now is the stillness that cradles your wisdom. Change is plotting your conquering, creature. Force will find you at every moment. Welcome its charge through your being. You are a calm wonder of divinity."

My hold loosened as an invisible force gently turned me right side up and instructed me, "Stare into it until it shifts. There's power in fresh eyes."

Drums pounded a hypnotic beat. These were the same percussive warnings that greeted me upon my entry into the forest. Vincent had called them Apollonian War Wolves. I followed the sound. The beats grew louder. Chanting rumbled through the glowing fires scattered among bodies shouting like mad animals into the night. Standing on a mound high in the middle was the woman from my past who had given me the tea. The one who had given the package to Ash in the woods. The wolf who brought me here. Ara. The moment we locked eyes, the drums and the noise came to an abrupt stop.

"Tell me, Red Crow of Justice, Moon Witch of the Wood, do you want to die tonight?"

The warriors erupted in deafening cheers as her eyes burned through me. She stepped off the mound and began to walk among the crowd. Her voice elevated, she continued with authority, "THE GLORY OF BATTLE IS THE MASTERY OF DEATH'S LINGER OVER SELF!

"AND SO IT GOES:

"THE WARRIOR WHO CREATED THIS INITIATION WAS CARRIED BY A WHITE HORSE ON A PATH OF FRESH SNOW. THEY TRAVERSED THE COUNTRYSIDE REVIEWING EVERY JOY AND EVERY SORROW KNOWN TO HUMANITY. THE WARRIOR REACHED THE END OF THE JOURNEY TO FIND A GRIM FIGURE DRESSED IN LUXURIOUS ROBES STANDING LIKE A TOWER MARKING THE END. FIRE BEGAN TO RAIN FROM THE SKY AS THE FIGURE SPOKE THESE WORDS:

"'ONE MUST GO THROUGH ME TO GO ON.'

"THE MESSAGE SUMMONED A WILD SMILE TO THE FACE OF THE WARRIOR. SHE COVERED HER EYES, CROSSED HER HEART WITH TWO BLADES, AND, IN COMPLETE TRUST, ENTERED DEATH."

Suddenly, the surrounding bonfires reached the sky, for only a moment. Their return to normal revealed a vanishing. All had disappeared except for Ara and me.

"Welcome to the beginning," she said.

"The beginning of what?" My tone was cold.

"The fire hidden deep in your eye screams Death. I can see the restraint in your shifting posture. War patiently waits inside of you."

I followed as she walked toward the woods. Every step she took was laced with caution.

"Are you going to continue this game, Ara, or can you get straight to the point?"

Ara grabbed her blade and pursued the rest of her point by charging toward me with unwavering confidence.

Instinct came swiftly, and I summoned my sword from the sky.

The clash of our blades produced a deafening ring in the air, rippling the ground and forcing it to open. The exposed earth womb claimed my body, and once again I found myself falling down a dark hole.

"When fear steals your breath, and darkness fills your sight, surrender to your shift, find safety in the flight of night."

Remembering the previous sea adventure, I allowed my shift. In my evolved state, my eyes saw a new earth unveiled. What was once dark was now a paradise of underground caverns. I flew through the tunnels. Higher elevations gifting streams of natural light near the surface sent memories of home to my heart. Mim's continual pour of love into my life was its own anchor. That resource gave me courage. I needed that nostalgia of home now.

As I flew deeper, my body began to tingle. The very air itself grew more alive as the cave grew darker. Suddenly, I wasn't alone. Staying the course, I continued until I saw a soft flame beckon in the distance. The pathway widened, revealing the source of the flame and my company. Her butterfly wings were light gray with soft accents of white. Black dots with orange centers scattered on her wings conjured the feeling of a thousand eyes staring back.

The fire looked warm and inviting. A few feet ahead, the earth opened to a bright sky. The breeze came in gently, with the light exposing a familiar burn in my belly. In my agony, the butterfly danced all around, weaving and spinning in delicate time. Her patterns enchanted me as the world began to slip away.

My senses were flooded with the smell of clove and black pepper. Alarmed, I jumped up to find I was no longer in my shift. There was no sign of the butterfly, only the source of the fragrance, which came from a pot cooking over the fire. No sooner than I became aware of the burn in my belly, a voice echoed from the shadow.

"Welcome to the initiation."

A being emerged from the dark with obsidian eyes and long, white hair. Her coal gaze gave way to an infinite sea of calm. The eyes, despite their colorless nature, captured a glimpse of the bridge between here and there. In a form otherwise human, she moved toward me almost without motion. I marveled at her allure. Pale-blue silk wrapped around her luminescent skin tone created neither a beginning nor end. I was both frightened and intrigued.

"Fear nothing in my temple, Emerson, for it is here you will begin your return home. I am the Harbinger of Fortune. Come."

Weary, I followed her through the dark just beyond the fire wondering what was in that pot.

"Medicine," she answered, as if she had read my mind.

"I did read your mind."

We approached a cavern, a few feet away sealed by a wall of vintage lumber. She walked to the left, through a dark-blue door that was propped open slightly. I followed, not prepared for the beauty beyond the earth's cavernous temple.

Marble floors with elaborate rugs greeted my weary feet as the sound of cascading water pulled my attention to the far end of the home. This was a palace hidden deep in the earth. The natural walls were painted white to bring light and breath into the space. An arrow pierced halfway through a pillow on the sofa, giving me pause.

"My lover is rather fond of arrows." A smile curled the corner of her mouth as the fondness of a memory found her face. "Come now, we haven't long."

We made our way down a long, open corridor revealing a massive waterfall. I felt myself recalling the caverns of home. Why did I feel so at home in the earth?

"Because you spent most of your battle crow life admiring it from afar. I have prepared a favorite from your past: Harren mushrooms with fig jam served with Sparrow Beach bread. That should refuel your energy and temper the burn post-shift." She gestured toward a sitting area.

"I am here to share a gift with you. The Carpathian Mountains contain an energy that goes beyond the understanding of its current occupants, even the Morning Star. Nevertheless, he felt its incredible pull and didn't need to understand it to build a sanctuary in its vortex of power. You are in my home beyond the veil now. That's why your shift was so hard on your body. I suspect it will continue to be a struggle until you become whole again."

I took one bite of the meal before me and was overcome. "What kind of food did you say this was, again?"

She laughed. "It's celestial steak. A rare mushroom found on Mars you would always pick for special meals. I knew you well, Justice, or whatever you are going by these days. But we're not here to discuss old times. Your company would have you believe that your recent awakening has started a series of events in motion, each push yearning to find truth and resolution to a mystery some still cannot quite fully grasp. The truth is, a darker power summoned your awakening with the help of someone near and dear to you. They hope to prevent your resurrection so that they may take control of the process."

"The process of what?"

"The process of cycling, or ascending. Pushing souls who are not ready beyond the veil will throw some of the higher realms into chaos. That is what the enemy wants to do. This forced vulnerability will expose the Earth and its place in the Universe. And just as we strive to keep souls from ascending too soon, your job was also to keep certain Divine forces from infiltrating the veil's younger side of evolution. Earth doesn't belong to any God or Goddess, yet some spend lifetimes trying to claim her, much like the God who captured your Morning Star, but that's an entirely different story.

"The Initiation in the Carpathian Forest is a path gifted to the warrior deemed worthy of finding a power boost laced in clarity. The land holds a quality that allows initiates to manifest their destiny with their current awareness and sort through shadow and power. It exposes the inner demons that hold them back from their highest potential. It also foreshadows what's to come.

"The average human would find this process gruesome and likely would not survive it without a strong dose of courage and blind trust. The Mid-Plane Mages like your battle crows, Solomon, Vincent, and others may struggle, but they possess the right amount of elevation to truly grow from its trials.

"Beyond the veil of origin exists other realms, each space with its own thinning. All spaces are hidden by transitional veils in the in-between on to the next. Just beyond this veil into the next realm are the Divine Wheels like me, you, Ash, and others. If we were to engage in this initiation in our purest form, it would change the very experience of Earth as they know it.

"Humans can choose enlightenment beyond what is easily known, but most don't. However, some of the ones who seek, much like your own enemies, are corrupted by their deity envy. There's a code, a supreme knowledge that comes from the influence of the environment we exist in. Nature shows us a natural rhythm unfolding all its layers in every living thing. We mustn't interfere with organic cosmic order.

"The world tips its chaos from one extreme to the next. Humanity continuously experiences what surrender and resistance in that energy does to your awakening. There are some humans who resist life for so long that they become detached to any familiarity of surrender and its promise of peace. They grow cold, creating an energy birthed from resisting.

"This cold covers them, leaving no room for giving, only taking. When a human roots into the energy of only taking, there is no space left to grow. The greatest monsters in life are ones driven by power created from a shadow with no connection to the majesty of surrendering to inner divinity. They spend so much time taking it from others they forget their own, becoming void of life. All the 'devils' in the world have nothing on the flameless ones moving through life with no inner light. Those are the real monsters of time."

My senses sharpened after the restorative meal. I began to find the sound of the water, at first calming, invigorating. I felt her lock into my thoughts this time.

"It's time," she said with smooth authority, standing to signal our time coming to an end.

"You will return to Earth. It will seem as if you were only gone one minute. This is how the initiation will unfold:

"The first task is the physical escape challenge. The Apollonian battle wolves, either in human or shift form, will try to wear you down physically. These warriors are trained specifically to protect the forest and its purpose. They will fight you with the intention of bringing you close to death. As they start to rush you, immediately orient yourself toward a path away from the mountain. Their aim will be to render you unconscious. Disappear before they get a chance to do so. Run away from the mountain. This advantage will grant you more time for the next task.

"Step two of the initiation process is simply known as night vision. You are shown only what you need to grow through this moment in time. The process can pull not only your truth, but also lessons currently being pulled to you. Focus on observing, not reliving.

"The final phase of the initiation is strength. You must lose yourself many times to regain the divine source of your origins."

As we made our way to the door, her gaze imbued me with confidence. It was an embrace through thought, wrapping the air between us in pure peace. I knew without words she was an important energy point in the Universe.

She stopped just short of the door. "It is your choice, Emerson. Your primary form identifies human, and that's where you must start. This door is no ordinary door. It senses your deepest desire and delivers you into that space. You have the power to choose to return to New Orleans, collect your grandmother, and return to the mountain, leaving this to be addressed in another lifetime.

"Imagine Emerson Buckley Stone, a simple life working in the family store. Perhaps you and Abel will marry or choose to go separate ways. You can spend the rest of your days studying humanity, rolling the dice on where all that may lead you in the end."

I felt the pull of temptation as I visualized an easier life.

"Or, you can make the choice that you have felt the fullness of this vibration and you're ready to move on to the next version of your existence. Just remember, it won't be easy. It will change you forever, in all ways. Free will is an amazing gift, but the results that fall beyond it aren't a guaranteed level of fulfillment. Regard every choice as precious."

I stood facing this door of destiny, unsure of what I desired.

"Logic isn't the only resource in the face of destiny. That's what makes choices tied to fate the most difficult. The magnificence of fate pulls you from the stability of logic and the trust that breathes in intuition. That confident surrender creates a loving space for fools to empty themselves for the new experience. You say you are unsure, yet your body is sorting out its desires every second."

Slowly, the door opened. A deep breath steadied me as I confidently raised my hand. The Harbinger looked at me curiously. "Why the hand?"

"To meet my sword."

The peace between us confirmed the accord in the Universe. I gave her a nod and walked into the next phase of my fate.

I emerged from the earth.

A surprised Ara braced reflexively. I rushed toward her, led by the point of my sword. To my surprise, wolves emerged from all sides, protecting their leader from my pursuit. The swift encirclement brought my inner Red Justice forward to every point of threat around. I fought everything that came for me.

A screech broke the sky, revealing a creature unlike anything I'd ever seen.

It was as tall as an ancient oak, with a body of what appeared to be metallic wood. Its face, replaced by a large opening, screamed its eerie cry all around. Every breath let out a shriek, bringing us all to an abrupt stop.

"We mean you no harm, Emerson," Ara called out from somewhere beyond the creature.

I took this stationary moment to assess my surroundings. War raged inside my being as the familiar taste of metal began to creep into my mouth. My shoulders began to shake, alerting me to my recent shift in space. Recognizing the coming transformation in the face of an unknown threat, I turned my back to the mountain to prepare my escape. My sword split in two as my wings began their painful push to the surface.

The creature breathed another call of war, and the dust of Earth began to rise. To protect myself, I crossed both swords over my heart just as feathers covered my face. The fabric tightened, pulling my hair. I had been blindfolded, stopping my shift cold.

Surrounded by silence, I could feel the presence of no one. My swords returned to the air as my human essence stepped, fully present, into my being. Immediately my hands reached for the back of my head, removing my blindfold, only to find upon its removal utter darkness.

Heal the human first. Human. The thought haunted my mind, knowing life as I had known it was no more.

Suddenly, I felt the need to move away from the open space. My inner eye opened with every inhale. In the distance, the faceless beast breathed another alarm in the air.

Had I moved that far away in a matter of seconds? Or perhaps there were more of these creatures.

Although blind, I could see color taking over my inner vision. The intuitive map manifesting in my mind's eye began to guide me further down the path, sensing things like density, temperature, and vibration. This cosmic lens quieted my quivering nerves, begging my human condition, for the first time in a while, to keep going.

Although courage carried my feet, fear had its grip on me.

The color leading my inner vision began to lose its natural flow. Orange and gold flashed, presenting a shape at a dead stop a few feet ahead.

"You have been here before, and many have come before you. We have an important message for you, Emerson."

The single voice boomed with subtle tones of many, sending chills up my spine.

"Don't bother looking for clarity. It must be earned."

The light reaching my mind's eye pulled me toward a water source. The shape hovered just close enough for me to sense its presence. I could see the extension of my light reaching towards the water source. My highest self knew what I needed.

Cool water washed over me, dropping my head, forcing my gaze toward my feet. The water, signaling a sudden awareness that my sight had returned, had me investigating its source. An iron chalice hovered in the sky, pouring a continual stream. I cast my vision forward, seeing the shadow come into fullness.

"The space you open here in this initiation can only be experienced by you and what you call to it."

When shadow covers thought, stand under the arching stream that pours from the iron chalice and cast your eyes down.

Mars-red hair engulfed her athletic presentation as she stood staring at me, unmoving as a mountain.

"We shared this space before, ages ago in other forms. I am Iris, carrier of truths among all realms. This space pulls visions to those who enter. Most pull ancestors or scenes through time. The more evolved may pull guides or animal spirits. You pulled me."

The chalice's pouring stream formed a pool of water between us.

"Tell me, Iris, what message of truth have you brought me?"

"It isn't about the words, Emerson. Divinity and all its infinite wisdom can't be reduced to two-dimensional interpretation, no matter its powerful influence. It must be felt, experienced, touched."

Her aura grew until the light that made her alchemized a rainbow between her vessel and the water below.

"This light will give you a loop of events that led exactly to this point in time. The distant future is chained to fate, but I can go a step beyond present to show you glimpses of developing futures."

She guided my hand to the colorful arch. Our surroundings began to swirl, and in the blink of an eye I found myself observing Saturn's final gate in a way that wasn't reflective of the place I had just been. I was observing this moment from another dimension through a filter of memories that I knew were moments I had already made in time.

"Because you are committed to journeying toward your human truth, you can only observe things not of this atmosphere. Your memories on Earth will be experienced in real time."

My concern for souls trying to ascend beyond this realm ahead of their own evolution heightened. Solomon arrived at his final moment of many trips to the veil with an unusual attachment. I disposed of the passenger and discovered an organization of men were trying to interfere with the natural process of the Earth ascension experience. Intrigued, Solomon vowed to incarnate one more time, along with me, to help resolve this disruption.

Our surroundings changed; disoriented, I realized I was in an old kitchen. A baby crying in the distance put my heart in my throat.

"Remember, Emerson, you must observe. Don't let it consume you."

Upon the return of my awareness, time moved forward, and my crying babe was older. A knock at the door broke my concentration, and the scene of my undoing began its unfolding. Again, time moved forward, finding me hanging, barely conscious. The medicine coursing through my veins made it hard to concentrate.

This scene had been presented to me in a dream, through a vision, and now through this initiation, all awarding me different perspectives on the situation. The execution team had their own motivations, but it was three gentlemen immediately to the left of my swinging feet whose conversation captivated me.

"Stick to the plan. Once the brotherhood has completed their mission, we'll steal the body. She's certain that once Solomon knows what's transpired, he will come for the witch."

He laughed. "However many pieces she ends up in."

The thieves discussed their plan of attack and how it needed to happen before the caravan reached the port. The vision Hagan and I experienced of Ash acquiring that finger, along with its precious ring, and assuring it was safely within the family was the best possible outcome from the chaos that was about to unfold.

A sweet smell overtook my senses. Time had revealed my childhood in Appalachia, a carousel of memories from a life that seemed most certainly to be the sweetest human life I had ever known. Suddenly, a rainbow of color cast the entire sky into a prism of artful magic.

Darkness blew the awesome sight from our eyes, revealing the pool reflecting these truths of old. Emotion couldn't find her face as I stood before her desperate to read it.

"I feel your desperation, friend. It is a sign the humanity is running strong within you. It is clear what brought you here, but shall we look deeper at what the source is requiring the attention of your destiny?"

The pool of water spiraled up in the air, projecting into a screen beyond us. A group of men sat around a table. The faces changed, yet the table stayed the same through the ages. Alternatively, I observed Solomon and other mages over the years in different incarnations, and it left me curious about their connection, that is, until I saw myself with Solomon running under the streets of Budapest. Clearly, during my previous life, he and I traveled far and wide searching very intently for something.

Scenes flipped between images of this table and its circle of importance to the wild, explorative adventures of Solomon and me. Rituals began to manifest at different locations, facilitated by familiar faces from the table. One thing was clear: No one in my current situation was present in these spaces other than Solomon, and he appeared to be my strongest ally yet.

Clove and pepper drenched the air.

A being with no eyes stepped from the shadows, carrying a small cauldron.

I thought to myself, the Harbinger of Fortune. "I know that medicine!"

Iris pointed to the creature. "This part of the initiation works with plant medicine. There's a variety to be found all over the Universe, and you pulled a source specific to your energy. Emerson, before I go, remember that you are fully integrated into your human self. There will be no more battle crow access, no more swords, no more shifting. Observe, but do not control. This forest is its own source of magic; it is up to you alone to find your way back."

"What do you mean? I can't shift? What about the others? How will I get home?" The panic consuming me was a painful reminder of the courage it takes to be human.

"You came into this world on a mission to be human. They did not. They came to support you. Utilize them. The grand path is discovered in majestic solitude, but exchange with the life surrounding you is what makes the journey bearable. We are always surrounded by everyone's version of alone."

As soon as I took the potion from the being, its form shifted into a swarm of ghostly white miniature moths.

Iris was gone.

A voice entered my head from the sky. I knew it came from the atmosphere above, because I felt the pressure pushing down on my ears. The vibration made my chest quiver.

"Drink into your soul the illumination of truth.

Awareness finds your clarity on what made you.

Visions expose what motivates you.

I am here to guide you, only if you are worthy.

Drink the medicine, child.

Drink.

Let it take you."

I drank.

CHAPTER 10

The Evil of Men

"He who is in possession of such sacred secrets controls the earth. We gather under the forces of the Universe with reverence to the evolution of soul. It is in this hour that we offer our sacrifice."

The ceremony revealed hundreds of people surrounding an enormous pit in the ground. Mechanical gallows enclosed the hole, creating a barrier between the ritual seekers and the horror. Operating the gallows were beings like the faceless creatures in the forest. The match would have been identical had the faceless void not been covered by a flat metal surface. Chains wrapped around their bodies, mirroring the suffering continually seeping from their imprisoned souls. An unpleasant, earthy smell overtook the room as an army of bulls was led to the floor.

The atmosphere sickened me. The only palpable emotion was despair.

Sound stepped in front of sight, guiding me more quickly to the horror I witnessed from the shadow. Fear painted the eye of every beast in the room. The energy of the frightened herd was harvested and consumed like food for the low vibrational mob. Feeding on the fears of others is only a false sense of power. Evil takes, no matter the cost.

The beasts never made a sound until the mechanical gallows snatched their legs, stringing them high in the air. Their woeful, constrained breaths heaved in sorrowful surrender. Their heavy bodies slammed to the ground before their rise to death. Animal sounds of tortured breathing filled the environment until the metal-face creatures cut their throats for the sanguine collection. Just as the bloodstream slowed, the gallows catapulted their bodies into the abyss. The ground pulsated in time with the receipt of each carcass. The sight of the power-hungry faces taking it all in was chilling, yet no more grotesque than the smell of massive volumes of blood.

Time moved on, showing at warp speed similar rituals using animals and humans. Through the ages, the mass sacrifices, creatures, and mechanical gallows were replaced with war rooms saturated in aristocracy, modern versions of their former hungry selves reaching back in time to the more antiquated behaviors of their foundations. Money replaced blood in their search for power. Desperately, they searched for meaning in magic that can now be surveyed with more intellectually evolved minds.

"Power is a resource often misused for control. The Pythagorean brotherhood is only a continuation of similar organizations influencing it from afar. The motivations of all willing oppressors may be in contrast to one another, but their endgame is to control the ascension of the consciousness of mankind.

"During the early stages of these gatherings, a unified aim of understanding brought seekers together from different corners of the world. Like all organizations of that magnitude, politics and greed pushed different chapters further toward their own agenda and away from a unified mission. Money created easier channels to acquiring rare items of power, and ancient knowledge became a resource for manipulation and control.

"Records exist of magic beings who walk this earth, but most do so hidden from the contamination of evildoers. Solomon came through so many times, chapter members began keeping tabs on him. This is being shown in your moment of truth because your interaction with Solomon in your first earthly lifetime put you on their radar."

My heart began to race as sweat poured from my brow. The energy extended from the trees, the ground, my fingertips, connecting our essence to the One. Medicine rushed through my system, influencing and enhancing every moment by the second. We all house a monster in our inner castle, and mine was awake and reacting.

"Now, you will be shown a glimpse of things to come."

My throat began to close. Gasping for air, I fell to my knees, clutching at the dirt. Scenes flashed so quickly it was hard at first to take them all in. Abel stood in a warehouse hovering over containers, holding a list of items in his hand. A map marking locations hung securely on a wall.

Labored breathing hijacked my concentration as one final scene played out before me. A ritual carrying the desperation energy of the previous slaughter unfolded, except this time a body lay on a stone slab as the sacrificial offering. The only exposed face in the crowd belonged to the facilitator. It was Victor Saturnali.

Just as the vision began to fade, I caught a glimpse of the ritual table. Adrenaline put me in a state of high alert. The medicine heightened my furious reaction to the revelation, and rage began to control the driving light that kept me alive in this world. I heard them coming for me in the distance. Sensing their desire to capture and conquer only deepened the madness within me.

A universal ring sounded, blowing the sky apart, rendering me numb. I could feel energy wrapped in words reaching me from another realm.

"Collecting the pieces of your past self is secondary only to exposing those who covet them."

Smoke began to manifest in pods all around, exposing portals from which two shadow figures emerged. I was in neurological overload, full of rage and empowered by the wickedness in the world that awaited me. Hands reached for me through smoke, but I met them with resistance and violence.

My fist slammed the face of the first being that touched my body. Through blurry eyes, I searched for the next figure and found its throat. I squeezed as hard as I could, controlling the life force of my trespasser.

"Mercy!"

"Emerson Stone!"

Voices of incoherent distress finally drew my attention. They were pulling at my body, trying to contain me. A familiar voice sprung a sudden grounding clarity in my midst. I found myself in clear view with the safest eyes I'd ever known.

"Hagan!"

He placed his hand over my heart, "Easy, Kentucky."

I stood up to find two more friends, Solomon and Ara.

"Good shot, Justice! You're lucky Solomon could see you in your human fullness. I was about to unleash my shift rage." She laughed, wiping blood off her shoulder that gushed from a cut in her cheek. "That ruby ring of yours is better than any sword you've ever wielded. Solomon can't hold the portals any longer. We must go."

Solomon's staff commanded a wave of dust that clouded all visibility.

"Stand still!" he commanded in thunderous echoes.

Dust rolled away, revealing the sky bridge in Solomon's realm in Carpathia. I ran to Hagan, holding him close.

"How did you get here?"

Before he answered, a familiar voice called from the distance, "After a few days of no contact, he insisted." Esther hugged me, pulling me close to whisper, "If you've seen Ash, keep it to yourself."

The energy storming from down the way carried her meaning before arrival.

"Calm yourself, Nyx!" Solomon cautiously walked towards his young apprentice, sensing her need for guidance.

"I opened space for you, you ungrateful... Do you have any idea what it takes to interfere with the majesty that is this cosmic sphere?"

She lunged for me, only to be confronted by Esther, who laughed in a playfully condescending way. "Easy, sister. As per usual, your reactions reflect your evolutionary needs."

Solomon stopped the mood cold. "Where did you go before the initiation?"

I remembered the beautiful memories of many shared adventures and meals in foreign lands discovering the mysteries of Earth. He and I surely shared a special friendship that, once remembered, will never leave my mind again. He stood before me, and although he had no idea what I was thinking, he felt it. I embraced him, holding him in a way that spoke a finality to the pause that life previously found us in.

"My friend. Yes, friend you and I have a magnificent history. We both misjudged humanity and dedicated many hours trying to restore balance. Let's take this somewhere more suitable. I have much to discuss with all of you."

Hagan and I lingered behind Esther, Solomon, and Nyx. I intentionally slowed our pace, driven by my need to know how he got here. He seemed incredibly unsettled but present all the same.

"Esther brought you?"

He wouldn't look at me. I worried my psychotic drug-induced journey work may have pushed him too far. Either way, he did not answer.

Solomon led us to a research room fit for a mad scientist and already occupied by Ara and Vincent. Nyx walked to a wall, revealing a secret entrance. Solomon the Wise breathed intensity that sometimes fell short of the light he truly is to this Universe. He carried more stories regarding the meaning of this existence than most beings realize, including himself.

I waited for them all to take a seat and then shared some of my recent revelations.

"We are here for a mission that reaches far beyond my personal journey. Before I continue, I would like to ask what you remember regarding our previous life together."

Esther stood, motioning for me to take her seat by Hagan.

"I am best equipped to respond. The Carpathian Battle Crows are a pack of moon children, one of many who protect this realm. We were raised together as a family with our mother, Selene. When you left Saturn to incarnate on Earth and eventually died in that lifetime, something happened to the Battle Crows. There were seven of us on Earth at the time of your death. All lost their memories except for Nyx, Ara, and me.

"The Carpathian Mountains speak fluidly among the realms of the Universe. This lends the mountain range the ability to cloak and protect many magic beings of Earth. We were all here, the rest with you out in the world. However, something else occurred during your death. Even the beings in the forest experienced a disconnect in their evolved knowing. It was as if a veil were lifted over all of us. I assumed the role of watcher to my siblings of Earth. Your mission here can be guided only on minor levels. I did what I could to watch over all of you."

I thought carefully about what I would tell them. It didn't seem appropriate to give them the full story, my story. My existence beyond battle crow was unknown to all who were present. With a deep breath, I began to offer them a glimpse into my knowing.

"During my time as battle crow, a great threat to the evolution revealed itself at the final gate. Souls were attempting to move beyond this realm prior to their evolutionary time. Their knowledge wasn't in alignment with their vibration. Fact seekers use knowledge as a security blanket, often unwilling to surrender to the truth of the connection that is the unknown.

"Solomon, I respected your wisdom and work towards your own evolution so much, I allowed you to recycle back to Earth consciously toward the end of your journeys. Upon your final return, a gate breaker tried to come through, giving me the final push to address this matter more personally. It was then that you vowed to return with me one final time to uncover the ones who are attempting to control the natural order of Earth's human experience.

"We are dealing with a group of humans motivated to control Earth and beyond, by hunger driven from their knowledge of mysteries of the Universe. They are working with elements, conjuring core magic from the earth. Solomon's multiple returns began to land on the wrong people's levels of recognition. Thus started conspiracy theories amongst certain fanatical seekers, which led them to our friendship and, eventually, to me. However, I am unaware of how much they know about me.

"My corpse was dismembered and scattered during transport. The forces behind it, I'm sure, are the very gate-breaking, grand-knowledge-seeking power monsters we're looking for."

"So, what's the plan?" Vincent's question softened Nyx's edge a bit. It was easy to see the faith in their love was more important than any emotions that might impede her forward movement.

In true Queen fashion, Esther interrupted, letting us know how she would be helping. "I'll be guiding the rest of our crow family back to the origins, just like I did with all of you. It will be up to them to see that path, but my aim is bold. If we're taking on a layer of the world's evil, it's probably best we team up as heavily as possible." She must be the oldest of the moon children, I thought.

I nodded in agreement. "Hagan, Ara, and I will return to New Orleans. I am no longer able to access my battle crow form until my pieces are recovered. My humanity is my resource from this point forward.

"Starting from what we know, we will work backward through the facts until we hit the original source. During the initiation, I was shown that my death pulled interest from more than one group of untrustworthy individuals. We will start there and work our way through the memories. Hopefully, in a short amount of time, we will have enough insight to evolve our plan."

"And me, old friend, what would you like me to offer?" Solomon, still cautious, had a light in his eyes that showed his readiness to see through something we both started long ago.

"I think it's best you all stay here, where you are protected, for now. I will drop information as I receive it in hopes you can utilize your resources here to further our efforts. Nyx and Vincent."

In a militant tone, Ara interrupted, "Nyx, you'll assume leadership among the Apollonian War Wolves in my absence. Prepare them for whatever your intuitive battle eye foresees. Vincent, keep your ear to the dirt among all the beings deep in the forest. The chatter will spread quickly through the magic community, as I'm sure they're feeling the shift of things to come."

"I'll book my solo flight home immediately, while Hagan and Ara will shift home via portal and prepare the aunts. I will be along in my own natural time."

"Absolutely not!" Hagan spoke for the first time since our return from the initiation. "Now that you're fully in your human timeline again, I can't leave you alone at your most vulnerable."

I laughed. I couldn't help myself. "Hagan, I have been a human navigating this world alone for some time. I can assure you this feels exactly the way my intuition says it needs to be. Besides, Ara can help you acclimate more comfortably to your shift, and maybe it will trigger more memories for your own origins."

Everyone scattered as I planned to fly from Bucharest to New Orleans. Booking on short notice left me with no other option but two layovers and a full day's journey home. I had had enough of portal transfer, so the time to reflect in silence seemed like a gift.

The closest town was more than an hour away. Vincent offered to drive me there and help me secure transportation to the airport. Hagan insisted on coming along. The trees were eerily still as we passed through the forest in silence.

A red church along the side of the road marked the first sign of life outside of the magic. Soon after, there were homes and, eventually, a town. Vincent had a local arrange for a car to the airport, 45 minutes away.

As the car arrived, Hagan pulled me aside. "I want to apologize to you for my silence. This whole thing still has me cautious of this new circle around us. Be mindful on your layovers for any possible suspicious followers. Please be safe, Emerson."

His goodbye hug pressed the necklace he gave me into my skin, reminding me Vincent had the same one. "Hagan, maybe talk to Vincent about this necklace." I tossed his protection amulet back to him, jumped into the car, and left for my return to the States.

Airport travel is so much easier with only a backpack. I reached into my pack for identification and discovered my cell phone. Once I made it through security, I found my gate and a place to charge my phone. When the battery regained enough power, concerned messages started popping up from Mim and Abel.

I called Mim to advise her of my travel plans. It would be three hours to Amsterdam, an hour layover, then eight more hours to Chicago. She let me know that Abel was frantic at first from not hearing from me. Apparently, she told him I decided to go to a spa and recharge with my cousin Esther. I would contact him as soon as I made it to the States.

The flight to Amsterdam passed quickly, but all the adventuring began to catch up with me. The next flight was an overnight, and sleep was the only thing on my mind for the second leg of this trip home. I settled into my seat, ordered a nightcap, and the next thing I knew, the captain's voice announcing our arrival woke me from a deep rest.

The customs area in O'Hare was full of weary passengers working through the motions of one station to the next. After making my way through, I was so focused on finding my next terminal I almost missed someone calling my name.

Almost.

"Emerson!"

It can't be.

I turned to see Abel Saturnali.

He grabbed me, so elated that the breath began to leave my body.

"Did I just see you coming from the international terminal? Your grandmother said you were at a spa?"

Isn't it funny how feelings step in front of everything logical we hold? One look at him brought my focus hard to the reality that was my human life in this current time. I traded the past few weeks of magic wonderment for a lifetime of comfort in what was known, throwing myself into his arms. I sadly felt the shift of a love once rooted in passion to fate. I took his hand and began to walk toward my terminal.

"My cousin Esther and I traveled to a spa in Romania. It was quick and unexpected, but so refreshing! How was Budapest?" I eagerly switched gears, hoping to gain some insight on his recent travel.

"Mercy, it's so good to see your face! I was so worried when I didn't hear from you. Maxine wouldn't say anything other than she would pass the message along. Aggie finally called me to let me know you went to a retreat in the mountains somewhere but, wow, I didn't realize somewhere was Romania!"

"I'll be sure to tell you all about it on the flight home to New Orleans. We are on the same flight, I'm assuming?"

"Actually, I'm going to Mexico. I need to drop off some cargo, and then I'll be straight home. I have a couple of hours before I board my next flight. Do you have time for breakfast?"

We made our way to a restaurant. Abel ordered coffee, eggs, and fruit for the both of us. He seemed different. He was surer of himself. Something happened on his trip that changed him; I could feel it. For that matter, something happened on my own trip that changed me, multiple times. I guess we never return from anything the same as before, and the further we go, the more opportunities to shift find us.

"So, tell me about your spa experience. Romania, what was that like?"

I spent the next several minutes painting a picture of a typical holiday full of pampering, dancing, drinking, and having fun. I explained that I had extended family who attended the ball, which prompted a last-minute reunion getaway.

"Budapest must have been magical. Was the trip successful? Were you able to obtain more pieces like that ritual cleaver you showed me?"

"It ended up being a bunch of old maps and books. Not what my father was hoping for, but I believe he was pleased all the same. The Parliament building was magnificent, lit up at night as the Danube River flowed in front, reflecting its beauty along with the moon. I thought of you."

His sincerity touched me, the way he always affected me. I could see now that primal need was not passion. That was only an illusion. The love was more casual than we cared to admit, but the lessons of shadow were the driving force here. It insisted on our engagement to become better versions of ourselves, even if that meant killing one or both of us in the process. We were in love with what our love served us.

His flight was to leave thirty minutes behind mine. We finished our meals and walked toward my terminal. I scanned his belongings, wondering whether any of the items were in his carry-on.

"What was the most exciting thing you discovered about the map? What were the books about?"

"The books were historical records, centuries old, from the brotherhood. As for the map, that, I have no clue. Originally, I was to meet a man by the name of Mr. Marton Fekete. He never showed for our meeting, and it was assumed he was no longer interested in doing business. My father arranged another buy with a former client in the area."

We arrived at my gate as the passengers started to board. I pulled him close to say goodbye. "Fate brought us together unexpectedly, Mr. Saturnali. Once again, those ships, they just keep passing by, don't they?"

"Better to be in each other's sights than not even in the same ocean."

The third and final leg of the trip was short compared to the rest of travel. I was surrounded by passengers with stories from all over the globe, all bound to their own missions, living numerous lifetimes in order to gain, what? Knowledge, awareness? The process of elevation could never be contained on the pages of any book. Words escape knowledge of this level.

I arrived in a state of tired determination. LJ was waiting at the airport in New Orleans to take me home. Her enthusiasm was enough to breathe a few more hours of life back into me.

"My mother won't tell me the entire reason you ended up in Europe. Being from this family, I understand there are things that are on a need-to-know basis. However, it is affecting all of us. I want to help. Plus, I miss you."

Sure, she was a believer. She was a wielder of earth magic; she sensed the shifting. But she was also loosely connected in such a way that she could live a more peaceful life. I'm sure Maxine felt she was safer if removed from the details.

"Well, Louisa Mae Jones, life has gotten a bit more complicated. What I can tell you is, we are sorting through it. The best way you can help is to continue living your life to the fullest. It's important we all linger under the radar for a bit."

I could see she wasn't satisfied with that answer. "LJ, you are the closest thing I have to a sister. I promise if there is anything you need to know, you'll know. So, tell me, who's occupying your heart these days?" I asked in an attempt to lighten the mood.

"Actually, now that you mention it, do you remember the girl I met the night you met Abel? The waitress from the diner, Inez? We ran into each other the night you came back to town."

"Oh, yeah? Are you thinking of finally planting some roots?"

"Slow down, Mercy. We've only messaged each other a few times," she said, laughing. "However, I pick her up tomorrow at seven!"

I loved the thought of LJ settling down into something traditional and loving, the perfect partner with a life far away from this.

As we drew closer to home, the pull to sleep grew more powerful. Auntie Maxine and Mim sat on the porch, creating the right complement to a humid late-summer evening. LJ dropped me off and left for work.

"Mercy!" Aggie held me close. I felt her love pouring into my soul, making sleep next to impossible to fight.

"It's so good to be back in the safety of familiarity. I have some ideas about where to start and wanted to get plans in place. Are Hagan and Ara inside?"

"We haven't had any visitors today, dear. Perhaps sleep is your best choice for now. We can discuss it all in the morning."

Aggie and Maxine settled me in for the night before returning to the house. Steam rose from my cup as the door shut behind them. I was alone with a heaviness that furiously battled my exhaustion. So far, this recovering had taught me the return continues to illuminate the inner alone. Origin, underneath the stripping away, presents to the weary an elusive ache of lonely. Lonely isn't the alone. The alone is the center. I needed to remember to reach beyond the illusion of the ache.

The sun gently touched my face, slowly opening my eyes. A peaceful H. Chambers Hoon was sleeping in a chair in the corner. I was relieved to see him. A noise turned my attention toward the front window, where LJ was stepping out of a car.

We made our way to the main house, finding Ara Greystone and the sisters in a spirited discussion about herbs. Breakfast, in its usual excess, covered every inch of the table. LJ made her way to sleep as we moved to the front room to discuss almost everything that had occurred. Certain parts were for my soul only.

We all agreed our immediate concern was Victor Saturnali. I explained my vision in detail, from Abel hovering over containers in a warehouse to Victor's human sacrifice. Maxine was angered by Victor's role in it all. His heavy involvement in the local community was a cause for concern in light of this revelation.

She was the first one to speak. "I will take it upon myself to work the information out of that weasel. After all, he and I have known each other the longest. The warehouse you saw was probably their business location on Canal Street."

"Actually, there's more." I paused before the reveal.

"As fate would have it, on my way back from Romania, I ran into Abel in the Chicago airport."

"You're just now mentioning this!" Chamber's voice was heavy with disappointment.

I shared what I had learned about the books and maps. The location could be local, but my intuition pointed to Mexico. Ara wanted to get her hands on that map. She was certain it would lead us to more clues. She and Hagan decided once the location of the warehouse was known, they would investigate it.

"Mim, I think it's best you go back home for now. I'll join you there as soon as it makes sense. New Orleans isn't the place for me right now. I need the power of my mountain."

"Center ground is the very thing we all need, however that looks to each of us."

I messaged Abel, asking if I could pick him up from the airport. He happily agreed and sent his flight information in return. The plane was arriving from San Diego, so Hagan and Ara immediately booked flights.

Ara handed me a phone. "Here, use this to communicate with us going forward. Try to find out anything you can regarding his whereabouts prior to San Diego. I'll touch base with you as soon as we land."

She gave Hagan a look that dared him to linger. That look told us she had knowledge beyond the awareness he and I shared.

"And, sister, one more thing." Grabbing my shoulders, she pulled me close. "I gave you the calming medicine because I could not bear to watch you suffer. I escaped to the forest for aid, but when we returned it was already finished. Trust was your downfall. Don't let it become the same poison this time." She continued to protect my mission no matter what. I could feel Ara was everything a true sibling should be: present, honest, and loyal.

Misting rain emptied the sidewalks. I held the look on Hagan's face in my memory. He didn't seem himself since our return. Himself? What do I know of who he really is, anyway? Instinct promised my safety with him, and that is all I really knew. Unlike Abel, who promised me the illusion of love through life's need to be relieved of itself. That drug is hard to put down. Even knowing what I know, the heat of anticipation flushed my face minutes away from seeing him.

I arrived at the airport to find Abel already waiting. There was a higher degree of confidence in his stance. He threw his bag in the car, hugging me.

"How was your journey? Was it a long flight?"

"It wasn't bad, just a few hours. I was so glad to be home."

We made small talk the rest of the way. He was tired, and I couldn't push for information yet. In the distance, I noticed a car in Abel's driveway.

"Are you expecting anyone?"

"That's my father!"

There was a change in Abel's ordinary tone toward Victor. His expression, once laced in boyish annoyance, had been replaced with rigid caution. Or maybe he was tired, and I was just paranoid. Victor's eyes locked into mine as I pulled in front of the house.

"Father. I wasn't expecting you."

"I know, I know. I was on the phone with your mother, and she relayed that Mercy would be bringing you home from the airport. I was working late at the office and thought I'd stop by since it's on the way. I left you a few messages, but you must have missed them. How was your trip?"

Mild tension surrounded the conversation, leaving me incredibly interested in Victor's motivation. Abel laughed it off and continued toward the door.

"The service across the border is spotty."

"I see." Victor's expression was empty. "Mercy, Abel tells me you've recently returned from some impromptu international traveling. Romania, was it? For a minute there, I thought you might have run after my son."

"My cousin Esther and I hadn't been around each other for quite some time. We decided to take a quick trip to catch up."

He stared at me for an uncomfortably long moment. "There are many fine spas right here in New Orleans. Why so far away?"

Abel interjected, "I'm sure any excuse to travel was enough for Mercy. She's a wandering spirit, this one."

"Wandering spirit," he chuckled. "Indeed. Mercy, we will have to get together soon. You can bring anyone you like. I'd be honored to have any of your family at my table for dinner."

The very thought of sharing a meal with that man made me shudder.

"That's very kind of you, Mr. Saturnali," I said, forcing a smile.

Abel walked Victor to his car. They were speaking in a low tone, but I could feel the conversation was strained.

As he entered the house, his irritation was clear. "Less than twenty-four hours without contact, and you'd think I was a child sneaking out of the house."

"Did I miss something? I knew things were tense between the two of you, but that was incredibly awkward."

"My father's focus has become increasingly forceful. It is like he's racing towards an invisible finish line. It all started when the client fell through. I questioned the deal's sudden importance. He responded with his usual excuse, 'staying ahead of the competition.' Apparently, this item was of the human bone variety, and arrangements had been made to get it legally back into the country. I guess the wasted time planning that didn't help his mood."

My stomach turned. I knew it belonged to me, at least, the old me. "Competition? Who are you competing against?"

"I don't want to take up all this time speaking about my father. I would much rather take this moment to enjoy time with you. It was nice seeing your face at the airport."

Abel hugged me in a way that I felt his truth. That didn't happen often with us. It wasn't that he was untruthful; we just resourced each other in other ways. The truth didn't matter like the present. Him standing here, tired from travel, frustrated, opened his light up to me in a way I had yet to experience.

I knew he had no knowledge of who I was, who he'd been to me through time. He was on a cycle of redemption. In this full state of human consciousness, my gifts insisted that fate had brought him to me for more than one reason. This relationship that once was all fire and no water suddenly started to take on a new life.

I decided to spend the night with Abel. I was reinvested in him, not just motivated by my mission. I found myself thinking that life, at any moment, is about one specific thing, but we truly are working infinite possibilities in everything we touch with just a single decision.

I started to unpack for him while he took a shower. There was the hint. The Universe always finds a way to put us where we need to be. A receipt to a hotel bar for a single drink in Rosarito, Mexico. I ran to grab my phone, took a screen shot of the receipt, and sent it to Ara and Hagan.

Location in Mexico = Rosarito. The failed item to be acquired in Budapest was a human bone. That's all I have. Be safe.

CHAPTER 11

Hagan

I have roamed this earth for more than a century, not knowing who I am. The theme throughout the first quarter of that time was anguish. My quest beyond that brought me the greatest clarity. I had been through my own evolution.

Mercy's message left more than curiosity lingering in my mind. A glimpse of that anguish I once held for my own story was surfacing through concern for her. We crossed the border from California into Tijuana just as the sun began to set. Rosarito was a short drive away. Vincent planned for us to have discreet accommodations as soon as we arrived.

"It looks like we're about ten minutes away. What are you thinking about? Hagan, are you ready, brother?"

Ara laughed at the possibility of anything. She was fearless, and I was enjoying getting to know my sibling. Our bond was instinctual; we were the same and connected. She taught me so much about my shift and how to navigate all of this in such a short amount of time.

"I'm thinking about how I wish we could have just opened a portal and flown here."

"Shifting is still new for you, and we can't risk exposing ourselves. Hagan, we will do everything we can to help her. And ourselves."

We pulled down a beach access road looking for Vincent's contact. The sun had made its exit, making identification difficult. The walled alleyway to the ocean was covered top to bottom in art. The path ended at the beach under a bright crescent moon.

"It's beautiful, isn't it?" Ara stared at the moon, lost in thought. "I hope to one day feel whole again. Nyx and I feel just as you do. No matter the varying degree to which we experienced it, the bottom line is we all lost something the day she died."

She turned around, looking past my right shoulder. "You must be Vincent's friend."

The warrior in her must have sensed his presence long before I knew he was there. I turned to find a gentleman with long, dark hair admiring an angel spray-painted on the wall. He stood there with his arms crossed, examining the piece.

"That detail is something, isn't it? I wonder how long it took them to create this masterpiece?"

He offered his hand. "Levi Rhodes. You must be Mr. Hoon and Ms. Graystone?"

"Vincent's friend?" Ara's tone was stern and direct.

"Oh no, ma'am. I don't know Mr. Black personally. I've been living in San Diego off and on for quite some time. Mr. Black introduced himself, explaining he knew about my predicament. He wanted to know if I would be interested in helping some people who were going through the same thing."

"Predicament?" I questioned.

"I'm assuming we're all quite old here?"

His laughter immediately invited in a familiar connection. Ara reacted in a way as if she had that very same thought and asked, "What's your shift color? Do you know your secondary?"

"What in the world are you talking about, lady? I'm a hunter."

"A hunter? What do you mean, hunter?" Ara was ruthless. I quickly imagined her in a full-on battle and was happy not to be on the receiving end of that intensity.

"I'm a contract hunter. Over the years I've made my living tracking animals and people for various employers. I woke up one day, with no memory, in the early existence of the town we know today as Old Town San Diego. I stumbled into a bar and was told my name and that I had just arrived looking for my sister, who had gone missing. I had no memory of any of it."

I gave him a friendly pat on the back, knowing I, too, had suffered the same alone: wandering the world with only a name, not knowing who I was. "We have quite a bit of catching up to do, Mr. Rhoads. Have you secured us a space to rest?"

"I rented a small vacation home not far from here. Shall we?"

We followed Levi to a Spanish-style beach cottage tucked away near the rocky coastline. Hours went by as we shared who we were, who he was. He insisted the missing sister wasn't Ara or Mercy but someone he knew was calling to him. Ara saw his persistence and supported his feelings despite his tale not making sense. Hell, nothing made sense anymore. But should it ever?

The next morning, I awoke to find that Levi had gone out prior to sunrise. He had collected information on three private warehouses in the area. We mapped out a plan and started the day at the first location. Each space turned out to be a dead end.

By midafternoon, hunger commanded our full attention. The streets of Rosarito were full of color and life. The soft sound of a violin called to me from around the corner. I felt a pulse surge through my body as I stumbled upon the source of such lovely sound. She was playing in front of a small restaurant called La Rosa.

The meal reenergized us, and we hashed out a new plan. A few feet to the left of our table, an older woman patiently worked with an oven on the open floor, making tortillas. She and Ara had been exchanging looks the entire time we've been here. Ara walked over to the woman.

They exchanged words and began to walk to the back of the restaurant. Levi and I followed them to a door leading to a cellar. Halfway down, a man stopped us from going further. The room seemed to be some sort of temple.

From below, Ara gave us a look that said she was more than capable of handling herself. "Hagan, everything's fine, trust me. I'll meet you both outside in ten minutes."

In exactly ten minutes, Ara walked around the corner. Before I had time to question how she left the restaurant, she ushered us quickly to the car. The car was dead silent as she raced down the highway. Levi and I, picking up the vibe, continually checked to see if we were being followed.

Once we were in the clear, I asked, "What was that about, Ara? Who's after us?"

"The woman in the restaurant is from a magical line of shifters. Sensing the urgency, along with my inner wolf, she tapped into my mind and spoke to me. I had only to mention a search for a predator of ancient magic in the area. She knew exactly where to send us. Her people have been tracking the threat for the past eighteen months. Apparently, this warehouse and its occupants are new to the area."

I sensed a half-truth within the words she presented. "Why did she take you downstairs? If she could communicate that to you at the table, why leave?"

"Clever, aren't you, brother?" Ara smiled, driving to a destination only she knew.

She turned off the main highway onto a dirt road. We drove for about five minutes before arriving at an open shed on the side of the road. A man stepped out, Ara paid him money, and then we continued along the road.

"Ara, what are we walking into?" I could tell she had a plan and was moving fast to execute whatever it was.

"If we hurry, we can arrive when the warehouse will have the least number of occupants. According to Anna, our friend at the restaurant, the day crew leaves at 3 p.m. That was thirty minutes ago. The warehouse is heavily guarded at night. The man we paid at the shed is a spy from her organization, working on the inside. She said there will be a pull-off as soon as the ocean comes in view. From there, we will travel on foot."

We followed the rocks along the coast until we got to a warehouse attached to a private airport. We snuck through the thick brush to the back entrance of the building. I looked at Ara, waiting on her cue, when suddenly Levi busted through the door as if he owned it. On the other side was an incredibly surprised security guard. He reached for a desk phone, only to be knocked out in two seconds flat by Ara.

Quickly, Levi taped his mouth shut and locked him in the closet. He took a tool out of his pocket, inserting it into the hard drive of the security system. He was able to rewind and pause the surveillance. On the other side of the door, we found a stairway going up to another floor.

"Hey Levi, how about you wait on my call this time?" Ara gave him a look that made it clear she was in charge of this operation.

Opening the door, we discovered an empty hallway leading to a handful of rooms. I noticed there were five doors.

"We'll split up, each taking a door. As soon as you discover anything, report back to the others immediately."

The first door revealed a storage closet filled with supplies and old office equipment. The second was a file room of documents, along with a couple of research desks. In the third room, I found them both examining a map. Some countries were flagged with key words:

Finland: Eyes

Hungary: Femur

England: Necklace

Romania: Book

Pictures of locations across the world were spread out on a board that called to mind an investigative crime scene. A framed piece of art hanging at the top center of the board called to me. It was a feeling I knew all too well. My own art speaks a language, and that picture was exuding remnants of similar magic.

Upon further investigation, I discovered it was an old canvas with monsters feeding on human flesh and script. It was protected and framed behind glass. The script said:

"Powerful control is gifted only when one consumes the righteous. Those who have no heart for true order. The eyes dismantle time; a whole head stops it. Spinal discs keep evil away. A femur assures sharp intellect. Feet connect roads carried through all your many lives. Consume the hearts and brains of pure children and old magic to further the spell of knowledge."

What was more disturbing was that the medium used to convey this message was paint on human flesh. I took a picture. Ara told us if they knew we were here, they would move everything. She didn't want to risk losing the opportunity to recover future items stored here. It had to be clean, in and out.

After we took pictures of everything, we started to leave. The sound of voices coming down the hallway stopped us cold. A team of scientists leaving for the day noticed a light on, as we hid behind a counter. They shut it off, closed the door, and left.

I looked at Levi. "What about the security guard? Won't they find him?"

"I would imagine they leave from another entrance, not the back."

Ara agreed with Levi. "We can tie up that loose end on the way out."

We made our escape to the back entrance. Ara took the guard's uniform to wear out of the building once the security footage resumed. Levi and I took our new hostage back to the car. The man's eyes were full of fear and desperation, but Levi never looked at him or engaged his spirit in any way.

The car was exactly as it was left, no sign that we'd been made. Levi threw our guest on the ground. He pulled a knife from his boot and charged the guard.

"What are you doing?" The second the words left my mouth, blood sprayed violently onto the earth.

For one moment I was speechless, then something compelled me to put my hands on the guard's body. I felt his soul pass through my being and into the cosmos. Enraged, I jumped up to confront Levi.

"Get rid of the body, and get in the car." Ara had returned, clearly unaffected by what had happened.

We drove in complete silence for thirty minutes. In my time of heavy sorrow, my heart drifted to Mercy. All this time alone rendered me capable of managing the ebb and flow of life. Hell, I did it better than most humans, but the minute my heart tethered itself to an external comfort I found myself dependent on the love of another. The need to paint emanated from the chambers of my pain.

"You and Vincent are so similar."

Ara's observation interrupted my thoughts, and I looked at her, urging her to elaborate.

"You both have the heart of an angel and the courage of kings. I see you share a similar talisman." She looked at my necklace.

"It makes sense that you two have history. The guard had to die, Hagan. He made the choice to work for an organization that didn't work out for him in the end. There are no easy decisions in war. Levi released him from his fear. Had he waited, his soul would have been even more anguished post-transition."

Throughout this whole mission, I never felt as weary as I did then.

✦

Tijuana was alive with tourists. Flashing red lights and parties under palm trees lining the streets relieved the dark ache. The border was packed with salespeople offering their wares.

"Churros!"

Levi's enormous laughter and hunger shattered the space where we all had been holding our breath. As we waited to cross the border, Ara sent the information and images to Vincent with instructions to make arrangements for our trip to Budapest. Levi and I would fly, while she went on ahead to search for our only lead, Mr. Marton Fekete. We needed to know why he missed that meeting and if he indeed had the femur mentioned on the warehouse map.

It took the better part of a day to travel to Budapest. Vincent had arranged for us to stay near the castle district of Buda in the hills. Our house, built into the cliff, faced the Danube River with the Parliament building shortly down the way. Ara was in the streets investigating when we arrived. She instructed us to take the next few hours to rest. Sleep called to us both, but I decided to check in with Mercy first.

"Hey," she answered. A simple word from her settled my unease.

"Hello, Kentucky." The fatigue was consuming me. "We finally made it to Budapest. Vincent has us in the most amazing home on the river. Ara's been in the streets for the past five hours searching for our guy. How are you?"

It was the kind of "how are you" that was laced with a need to know more from her than I had earned the right to.

"Things are calm. Since my grandmother returned to the mountain, I'm staying close to Maxine. We are doing all we can to maintain the appearance of an ordinary day. You sound exhausted. Are you OK? Vincent told me about Mexico."

"I see news travels fast in this family." Much to my surprise, she was already in the loop. I somehow felt embarrassed by my compassion for the guard. She was this grand battle crow. Nyx, Ara, and Levi clearly possessed those same violent tendencies. I was keenly aware that I am not made the same way.

As if reading my mind, Mercy, clearly trying to comfort me, said, "You're a healer. A warrior of hope."

But there was pity in her voice, and I didn't want that, not from her. "How's Abel? He hasn't tried to kill you?" There, I said it. I needed to know where she was with him, and what he knew about all of us. I knew deep down that if she had information relevant to the mission, we would all be aware. Still, it was not enough for my ego to accept that.

"I'm convinced he's unaware of the details of his father's dealings. Victor, on the other hand, has to know something."

"What makes you say that?"

"He was waiting at Abel's house when we arrived a couple of nights ago. I don't like the way he looks at me. It is as if he knows something, and he wants me to pick up on that fact. He didn't say anything out of the ordinary, but I definitely have my eyes on him."

I stuffed my reaction down. "Let us know if anything surfaces. We'll be back as soon as we can."

She was the strongest being I'd ever encountered, and fate seemed to be on her side this time more than the last life. I was motivated to solve this mystery for many reasons. I would be lying if I didn't say one of those reasons was exploring my connection to her.

My room was in the basement. The cool earth provided a den-like atmosphere, making sleep harder to escape. Just as I was about to close my eyes, I heard cracking noises coming from the wall. A bookcase slid to the left, and Vincent emerged from a secret passage.

Without stepping to the surface, he said, "Let's take a walk, friend."

The stairs were handmade and uneven at times, making them difficult to navigate in the dim lighting. My eyes adjusted as the cold damp air revived my senses. "I thought you couldn't leave the forest."

"It's not that I can't leave. I shouldn't. I am half-human, half-celestial. There are many parties interested in exploiting the gifts of my kind. The forest keeps me shielded from their senses. If I do venture outside of those sacred trees, it's never above the earth's surface. The cave systems of this Earth have their own separate world, and it's unlike anything you could imagine.

"Ara told me about what happened in Mexico. I came to see you, and to bring you this, of course."

He handed me a vile of thick green liquid.

"What am I supposed to do with this?"

"Drink it. You put your hands on the man because he died as a result of spiritual warfare. When souls reach the end, their transition into the next life is a result of how they energetically managed this one. If you leave in a state of chaos, the soul lingers, holding on to the past wanting the impossible, a redo. When the energy is finally available to move on, the vibration is so low that their next incarnation takes them several steps back in the grand journey.

"When you laid hands on the physical body, it comforted the last chord tethering the soul. You facilitated a space of higher vibration for him to move forward. You sent him further than he could have gotten on his own. You manipulated his ascension."

"Isn't that the very thing Mercy's trying to stop? I interfered with the natural order."

"Beings have always interfered with cosmic order. We react. If there were set rules operating on autopilot, there would be no growth. Drink. I know so much about this because it's my gift. I must have taught you in our time together."

"It would explain the talisman we share, I suppose." I grabbed the rings hanging from the necklace and devoured the concoction. As we continued to walk, I immediately felt calm wash over my mind and energy fill my soul.

"It would explain this, too." Vincent pointed to a mural painted on a wall underground.

"Did I paint this?" It was remarkable. A city burned from the wrath of fiery dragons in the sky. What took my breath was the beauty growing underneath. It was an underwater civilization rising to freedom.

He laughed. "No, but I see how you might think that you did. I painted it hundreds of years ago. I had forgotten until my journey here to see you and discovered it before arriving at your room. You see your presence in the mural because you were present the night it was created, guiding me patiently.

"It would appear we influenced each other with our talents. I came to tell you this in person because of the very thing you just said. That gift is a small interference with the natural order. I told Ara it's a way to honor the dead, although I'm certain she didn't believe me.

"The understanding of meddling with what is perceived as natural order is a limited way of thinking. And all the same, humanity, for the most part, is too corrupt to manage that available resource. I have not been completely in the dark as you have, friend, but I am eager to uncover my own truth now. It would seem we're all searching for pieces of ourselves."

Ara sent a message that came through simultaneously to each of us.

I found Fekete. Meet me at the castle on the hill in 20.

"You go ahead with Levi. I'll head that way underground."

The streets of Budapest were congested with traffic and loud with angry horns. Levi did his best, but we still arrived late to an impatient Ara.

"It's about time, you two. Marton Fekete is a librarian at the University. He comes to this pastry shop every evening before walking home."

"I'm getting a pastry." Levi left without hesitation to procure a sweet treat.

"The man has a sweet tooth, apparently." Ara laughed at his lack of focus or concern.

I was learning that Levi was a kind of go-with-the-flow type of soul. His energy wasn't loud on the surface, but he could kill in a second without a thought.

Ara casually started following a tall man with large black-frame glasses down the street. I stayed a few steps behind her with Levi, croissant in hand, a few steps behind me.

Mr. Fekete was fumbling through his keys as he stopped in front of a door. The second he turned the knob, Ara forced him through the door. We walked into the small apartment space, Ara with a knife to his throat. Fekete shuddered at the sight of Levi as he locked the door.

Ara questioned him repeatedly about the meeting, and he refused to cooperate. Levi started to ransack the place, finding research on ancient artifacts and spiritual organizations all over the globe. Ara, amid her interrogation, spotted a drawing on the kitchen table at the same time Levi picked up the picture beside it. The drawing was of a crow. The picture was a woman with long black hair and a face similar to Levi's.

"Pearl!" Levi rushed Martin in a fit of rage. "Where's my sister?"

I grabbed Levi as Ara protected the life of our informant.

"What bone were you to bring to your meeting with Apollo Industries? Where's Pearl?" Ara held the knife back to his eyeball as extra encouragement for truth telling.

"How do you know Pearl?"

"That isn't what I asked you, Mr. Fekete. You have thirty seconds to respond, or I'll start removing things, starting with this eye."

Shaking, he replied, "Pearl is my girlfriend. She's been missing since the day before yesterday. She arranged a meeting with a company she'd been researching. She sent me to feel them out but said the man who came wasn't who she was expecting. We bailed. I told her this would backfire!"

"What research?"

He stared, unwilling to respond until blood began to pour from where the tip of Ara's knife penetrated the skin just beside his temple. "OK! OK! Pearl doesn't age. She has no idea who she is or where she comes from. She's desperately been trying to find out about her home. A voice called to her, and she obsessively studied to understand who might be on the other side of it. Now I see that it's you." He looked at Levi, whose anger softened.

I held my hand out. "I'm Hagan. These are Ara and Levi. We need to find Pearl and the item she promised the Saturnalis. We believe it is the answer to her mystery and ours."

Fekete cautiously looked around, as if to make sure we were truly alone. "A man came by yesterday asking about the package. I explained to him that I was just a courier and gave him the fake alias and business Pearl works under. I'm sure it's only a matter of time before they realize she lived here with me."

He disappeared into a back room, returning with a black box the size of a telescope. Inside the box was a human leg bone.

"Here, take it. I am sure it's just a matter of time before they come back for me."

Ara gave the box back to him. "Hang on to it. You have five minutes to pack a bag. You're coming with us."

"Ara, we can't take him back to the States with us. That's just going to slow us down." Levi's voice was saturated with desperation. His nonchalant manner had fallen to the wayside.

"We're not taking him with us. We're taking him to Vincent, and all of us are returning to the forest. Marton, the bone, and Pearl's research will be safer there. Vincent can make arrangements to get us back to the forest through the underground."

A message came through on Ara's phone, giving the signal it was time to move. One of many entrances leading to underneath the streets of Buda was around the corner a couple of blocks away. Levi verified that the coast was clear, and off we moved, careful to stay out of sight.

We stopped by the house via the tunnel system to gather our belongings and more lanterns but swiftly resumed our mission. After an hour of walking, the path became so narrow it was impassable. Vincent turned a rock on the wall that opened a secret passage deeper into the earth.

"I made a trade with the conductor to allow nonstop travel in a private car on the rail system. This passage will be discreet and quick. The line ends in Slovakia near the highest peak in the Carpathian Mountains and my oldest memory of home. Solomon will be waiting with a transport to take all of you farther into the forest."

"All of us? Will you not be coming with us, friend?"

"I'm going to make a stop to see a trusted old friend. If things get out of hand, I believe we may need allies." He placed his hands on my shoulders. "Always follow your instinct, Hagan. And remember, the things that set us apart from the group are the secret weapons we use to thrive in life. Stay with what feels right, always."

After all this time alone, I thought peace in solitude made me free. To a degree, navigating the alone does make us free when managed consciously. However, Vincent taught me that the influence of everyone's alone deserves an audience. Freedom needs a space to react to and from, to remember who it is inside of us.

Chapter 12

Dinner Party

The Saturnalis' family home was just outside the city. Abel's father insisted we be there promptly at six. Victor was a man who always needed to be in control of his environment. Abel was so caught up in work, our time had been limited. I had my guard up but was also ready to find out anything I could in the few hours we would be there.

This week, I found myself investing into my old life. I started losing my connection to everything I had just worked for. This thing Abel and I shared with fate was so heavy it pulled me into the illusion of seeing this single event as my whole story. Now that I had experienced my essence in elevated forms, I saw how very human it is to compartmentalize the higher self.

"Mercy, thank you for being in my life."

That was out of nowhere. "What's going through your mind, Abel?"

"This new position wasn't at all anything I thought it would be. I am not happy. Research in solitude is where I thrive, but my father always had his way. I have no choice but to take up the family business more assertively, as he put it. I appreciate you because you have no expectations of me."

"You are freer than you think, Abel. This is not the way it has to be. You can choose differently."

"Maybe someday you'll make me brave," he said, laughing.

Just as he said that, we arrived, and the combination put a chill in my heart. He parked the car next to a bed of irises. I opened my door, and as Abel exited his side, I heard a familiar voice in my mind.

"Hide the ring!"

I quickly pulled my ruby off my finger. I placed it on the long chain around my neck and tucked it into my shirt. That quick connection to Iris brought my mission back to the forefront of my mind.

Music floated from the open entrance of the main home. As we entered, a contractor was hanging a picture in the center of the foyer that stopped me cold. Abel tugged on my arm, trying to keep me moving, but I couldn't turn away from the picture.

It was a photograph of a woman bound in a solid white empty room. Her eyes were full of rage and pain. Despite her vulnerable position, it was clear she was a warrior. This woman, covered from head to toe in tattoos, with hair dark as night, gave a look that promised revenge, should opportunity strike.

"Do you like my new art? Fascinating, isn't it, Emerson? I just acquired it today."

While I was mesmerized by the painting, Victor had entered the room.

"I think it's aggressive," I replied. I was familiar with certain styles of erotic rope art, but this was different.

His laughter echoed through the grand room. "Aggressive, you say? In what way?"

"It feels restrictive, desperate, and wrong."

"Abel, why don't you go on and say hello to your mother, and Emerson and I will be right along," he ordered. Then he immediately returned his attention to me and the picture. "Where do you see aggression?"

"In her eyes."

He moved uncomfortably close to my body. "Perhaps you see what's on the surface, Emerson. A woman who is restricted, possibly against her will, confined."

"Possibly? She's in pain! Her rage is palpable." I could feel his breath on my cheek.

"You see rage. I see wild. It is possible she's incredibly aware of her burdens as much as her wild. Sometimes people put themselves in situations to tame the beast within. To be controlled is a gift under the right circumstances. Shall we?"

He offered me his arm, and my stomach began to churn. I forced a smile onto my face. Victor was a hard read for me. He couldn't block his energy like Ash; it wasn't a purposeful protection. He was chaos and power. His ego breathed so loud, it was as if it was intentionally hiding some of the truth.

Abel and his mother Joan were in the dining room having a drink. I didn't know her well, but she seemed more like Abel than his father. She was quiet. I suppose being married to a man who is loud in every way leaves little room for anything else.

"Emerson, please overlook that awful picture my bizarre husband purchased," she said in a casual tone. "I only entertain his extremes because I know they're rarely permanent. Come, dinner is ready!"

Conversations at the table stayed anchored in business. Abel's father was a talker and happy to speak about the artifacts of varying origins he hoped would one day put his division of Apollo Industries on the map. Of course, none of the conversation reflected anything of interest to my cause.

"Emerson, since you have quite the travel bug, maybe you can travel with my son next time. Abel has more trips coming up soon. It might be the very thing he needs to get a little more enthusiastic about his new role."

This was my opportunity to pry. "I would love that, Mr. Saturnali. My goal is to see as much of the world as I can. Make sure you send me on the trip with the rarest item."

"Tell me, Mercy, are you knowledgeable of sacred items?" Victor asked. "Are there specific things you're drawn to?"

Strategically, I answered the way Mercy the healer from Moon Ruth Hollow would. "I suppose I'd love something in the realm of healing arts. Like maybe if there were any sort of healing talismans to be found. I don't know. I think that would be neat!"

"Tell her about our artifacts relating to past lives. You mentioned something about that recently, didn't you, Mercy?"

Abel naively offered the statement without noticing that it immediately changed Victor's disposition. He stared a hole through me and said, "Emerson, I didn't really take you for the reincarnation type."

"I haven't really given it much thought," I lied. "I told Abel our love must be continuing from a past life because we seem so strongly connected."

"I see," Victor replied.

"What would you say is the most powerful healing stone on the planet?" I asked innocently.

"That's not such a simple question, Mercy. You see, it's not necessarily the type of stone that determines its power. The most powerful stones are the ones that hold the knowledge of their source of origin. There are layers of vibrations in stones and talismans, and if you get an item close to its source of origin, you can access its full potential." He paused, wanting me to consider his words carefully. "I have something along those lines you may be interested in."

"Oh, goody." Something told me I wasn't going to like where this was going.

Victor led us down the hall into a den. Abel went to make another drink. He clearly was on autopilot around his father, stuck in some space of half present and barely coping. In the left-hand corner of the room, Victor stood proudly by another picture, this one a painting of a ghostly woman.

"Oh, no, Victor, not more discomforting art!" Abel's mother exclaimed.

"Joan, this isn't an ordinary piece," Victor said, coldly. "It comes with a story. A self-proclaimed magician said this painting had been in his family for more than a hundred years. The artist is unknown. They say the woman's heart turned to stone because she held more love inside of her than any being in the known Universe."

The painting was haunting. "Why would love turn her heart to stone?"

"Perception is everything. The red light you see emanating from her heart space is a ruby. That is the stone that claimed her humanity. Some say the story is real and the ruby heart is somewhere out in the world. But I haven't really given it much thought."

Victor's use of my own words back to me did not go unnoticed – and he knew it.

My humanity had taken over at this point to such a degree that the mention of the ruby left me shaken. I started to feel faint, and all I could think was, No, not here. Victor absorbed every moment of my discomfort with restrained pleasure. His last statement was a warning. However, his ego was so great I was certain that if he truly knew something, he would have said it.

"Abel, bring Mercy a drink. She's looking a little pale, and whiskey is always such a good pick-me-up."

At the mention of my possible distress, Abel was at my side in a minute. A drink was exactly what I needed. In fact, the whole bottle would be even better. Luckily, the drink grounded me enough to find my power.

"My apologies, I lost myself there for a minute. I've not eaten very much today. Maxine and I did a lot of work around her house today, and throughout that whole process I neglected my self-care."

"That's easy to do when you're putting in a good day's work," Victor replied. "How wonderful it is for Maxine to have you around. Louisa's unpredictable work schedule probably doesn't allow her much room for support on those types of things. What about your grandmother? I'm sure she loves being closer to her sister."

"My grandmother is back home now in Kentucky." His mention of LJ and Mim made my stomach turn.

"We should probably get you home to rest, Mercy," Abel interjected

Abel used my episode as an opportunity to leave. He was ready to go as soon as dinner was over, anyway. We were making our way through the house when Victor suddenly paused at the entrance to the kitchen. He instructed us to wait there for a moment and dipped into the room, returning with a snack.

"For the road. To help with your queasiness."

"No, thank you. I'm sure I'll be fine."

"Oh no, please, I insist. The crackers and meat are pretty standard, but the assortment of cheeses is of very high quality."

Leave it to this man's eccentricities to make cheese and crackers offputting. If it meant getting out of this house, then I would happily eat the damned snack. We said our goodbyes, and as I passed the irises to get into the car, the voice returned, except this time it sounded farther away. I wasn't sure if it was Iris. It said:

"Your system is unclean."

Late-summer sunsets in New Orleans filled the sky with erratic shades of fire. Abel spent the entire drive home ranting about his father's arrogance. Something had changed between them since his trip. He no longer whispered his feelings about him like a boy. It was as if they were almost aware of each other for the first time. As a result, Abel was awake now and more willing to speak his needs from his own personal power.

There was only a moment of light left in the sky when he pulled in front of Maxine's. I saw him with new eyes in that last bit of day. As angry as he was, I could still sense he wasn't as lost as he used to be. We both had shifted from this space of aimless uncertainty to reaction energy, navigating spaces now filled with a new purpose.

"Mercy, I admire how you are with him."

"Who, your father? How so?" As soon as the words left my mouth, the image of the bound woman flashed into my mind.

"You never show fear, always facing all things with confidence. Do you have some sort of secret power?" He laughed.

"What are you afraid of, Abel?"

"He wants me to be like him, but his passions aren't my passions. Yet, here I am, a grown man doing everything he tells me to do. My mother has tried to convince me that my discomfort is due to the fact that the work is new. She told me to give myself time to adjust to the change of pace. You would never let someone tell you how to live. You're free."

The light was no longer present in the sky, and my heart sympathized with his sorrow. However, there's power in choice. He and I had had this same conversation in other ways about his circumstance. The old Mercy would have loved him through it, but the enlightened Mercy saw this was his quest. We're all on our own mission, and sometimes as we evolve our quests either bring us closer together or push us farther apart.

I leaned over and kissed his cheek. "I believe in your ability to choose what's best for you. Look to the deeper truth. Reaction is big for you right now, and it's screaming, 'See! See this thing here that makes you react. Why?' The honest answer is the first step towards freedom."

He left, seeming slightly down from the events of the day. In the past, we would have gotten lost in each other's chaos, but that space between us had evolved into a more cautious area. The distraction of his mission pulled me so far away from my own.

Suddenly, another image of the bound girl appeared in my mind's eye, except this time the image was in real time. I took a deep breath, willing the thought to disappear, not wanting to entertain anything connected to that man. I'd had enough of that weird today.

Walking down the alley toward my cottage, I caught an old, familiar smell. Auntie Maxine sat on her back porch, clove in hand. "Child, there will come a time you'll have to let him go. Best you get that fixed in your head now."

"Any word from the crows?"

"Nothing since Vincent called for you yesterday. How was dinner?" Her tone was short.

"Dinner was full of Victor Saturnali and all the things he felt the need to express. The only takeaway was a painting he shared — a woman whose heart had turned into a ruby. I'm certain it was a passive way of warning me. We can't know for sure what he knows, but I can feel it's something."

She was distracted. "We will see what the cards have to say about that in the morning, but for now I think it's time to call it a night."

"You OK, Auntie Max?"

"Don't worry about me, child. Rest, my love."

My little home in New Orleans didn't hold the same amount of excitement as it did when I first arrived. My energy was calling me everywhere but here. I was looking forward to meeting back up with the crows. I could not imagine the gentle sweetness of Hagan with the intensity of Ara. The thought made sleep come easy for me.

A ringing in my ear disorients me from my surroundings. Sounds are echoing, fading in and out with no specific vision of anything in sight. I feel sick in my own skin. I've traveled through portals in the ocean, sky, Earth, space, all extreme, yet not nearly as dark as this experience. The previous spaces were full of life, yet this is far removed from anything touched by divine surrender. Things don't grow well in spaces like this.

The mess of colors begins to take shape. Chains rattle, pulling everything into focus. A white room so bright it is blinding flashes in and out of sight, showing me glimpses of the bound girl. Each flash of the scene at hand is a broken movie of violence and madness. In the beginning, she lies helpless, disconnected from reality as the gang of masked men lay their evil in her. Another flash reveals a woman dressed in gold wearing a dragon mask observing the gore.

Dragon lady holds her hand up as the last knot is tied around the woman's beaten body. She proceeds to take photos of the woman as if she were an object void of feeling. She is no object, though. The broken girl at the beginning of this horror has a fire in her eyes that is growing bigger by the minute.

The woman begins to squirm while a man wearing the head of a bear walks towards her. The room empties, leaving only the two. He straddles her bound body and begins to pull her hair away from her face. Tears run down her cheek, which serve only to encourage her torturer's longing.

He reaches down into his boot and pulls out a knife. She has no time to react before he slams her head into the ground, cutting a piece of the tip of her ear. Without hesitation, he eats it and begins to degrade her body. I choose to immediately forget.

Thunder boomed through the sky, and I bolted out of bed. I had been so disturbed by that image, it was haunting my dreams. As soon as I got out of bed to make some tea, the electricity went out. So much for that. I looked out the window, noticing the whole neighborhood had lost power. Well, whiskey is as good as tea, I thought.

I took the lantern from the back bedroom down the hall and noticed something in the mirror. Rather, I noticed something was missing: my reflection. I mashed my eyes tightly closed, then opened them again hoping to find I was mistaken, but this time, the mirror was black. A whirlpool manifested, revealing the scene from my dream.

The man in the bear mask was dancing like a lunatic. He fell to his knees, drunk on power, shouting chants into the night. In a moment of reverence, he removed the mask, lifting it high in the sky. The identity of this filth was none other than Victor Saturnali. The mirror had one final offering before returning my reflection: a view of the Saturnali kitchen.

Morning came, and I eased my eyes open. That picture really got under my skin. Such an odd dream. I got ready to head over to see Max and maybe LJ if she was home. She was never there anymore now that she had Inez. It was sad. With everything going on now, it wasn't the time to entertain strangers. Unfortunately, that meant it would be a while before we could get to know her new love. The result of this was LJ spending more time away from home.

Just as I was about to leave the house, I noticed my lantern on the counter. Last night wasn't a dream! I ran to Max's house and told her every detail. I expressed my concern with how the feeling of not being in my own skin was haunting me. She took me to her ritual room in the attic to see what she could deduce.

Auntie Max only shared magic with me a few times when I was a young girl. She was nothing like her sister. Mim cooked and nurtured, using the land to enhance her manifestations and help others. Maxine was a different bird. She was a grand magician, a manipulator of elements and beings. The type of magic she practiced was more consequential. She understood the emotional sacrifice of soul evolution and its mistress, humility — a power couple that must stay in balance or fall to self-destruction.

"Lie down, Emerson. This process isn't pleasant, so I fixed you a tincture to ease the blow."

"Ease the blow? Is it painful? What are you going to do?"

"The problem at hand is your visions of the enemy. They didn't gradually come like intuitive waves. They came in intrusive force after an evening with him. That's the root I aim to dig out. And I do mean dig. I'm going into your mind, to the moment you entered the Saturnali home."

She began to chant in sounds, not language. I drank the tincture, instantly floating into the scene as if I were reliving it, but this time removed of emotion. I made it all the way through the night until the moment came for us to go. As soon as Victor stepped into the kitchen, I became violently ill. I lost the vision as sweat poured from my body.

"Ah, there it is." Auntie Max stopped chanting. "This is where we go deeper."

She began blowing on various parts of my body. Heat slowly built into my system until my insides burned like a wildfire. The temperature consumed my presence, throwing me into a vision of Victor sitting alone at a dining table. It wasn't your ordinary meal with the family. A circle of people dressed head to toe in gold silk-hooded robes encircled him. Dishes were draped about on platters surrounded by laurel and bones. Victor drew his knife, shaving a piece of flesh from his arm. He placed it on a plate, sending it out of the room.

My discomfort increased as the scene shifted to the vision I received during the initiation. There were so many people who exuded wealth from their very appearance. I focused on the ritual altar only to find the bound woman who had haunted me since I first saw her. The scene faded like water rushing down a drain, slowly whirling away from me. The last moment revealed a snapshot that sent me spiraling. The snack made just for me had Victor's skin among the ingredients.

Auntie Maxine placed her left hand on my stomach, giving it a gentle rock. My insides began to twist and turn until I turned to the side, violently vomiting. Ease washed over me as Auntie Max began to open the windows to allow the morning light to flood the room. She sang classic rock songs, utilizing the sound of familiar rhythm to continue holding the space in power and renewal.

She left me to recover in the power of the sun's first light. I felt stronger and angrier with every passing second. Victor was psychotic, and I had to stop his madness. I wondered what Hagan's reaction would be to it all. He was such a champion for healing the soul. I wondered what he'd think when I asked Ara to help me kill Victor.

Auntie Max stood over a pot of water, lost in thought. There was something going on with her that started before I came home last night. The eccentricities that had you seeing way past her age were put away. She wore her later season in life like a heavy coat, as if the bitter chill of whatever stole her spunk would kill her.

"Auntie Max, what just happened? Please tell me what's weighing on you. What are you not saying?" I wondered if she was picking up on my homicidal rage.

"So, you want to kill Victor?" She laughed. "That isn't what's anchoring me, child. I feel the winds of hard change breathing through all my divination as of late. Victor's reach extends beyond the city of New Orleans. He has a hand in magical organizations all around the globe. Victor Saturnali may wear the face of the villain today, but he represents something larger than he's capable of managing alone."

We both jumped at the sound of knocking at the back door. I opened the door to an eager Ara and Nyx. Auntie Max hugged Ara like she was her own. Those two had bonded over the harshness of their turn, no doubt. Ara introduced Auntie Max to Nyx, who also packed a rowdy punch. Max was among women who carried feathers similar to her own, so to speak.

"Where's Hagan?" I caught myself asking in an overly obvious, non-casual way.

Ara, amused by my lack of tact, replied, "Your precious Hagan stayed behind with Vincent to run one more lead. Esther and Levi are on their way as we speak. We have so much to tell you!"

"Well, your timing couldn't be any more perfect, because I have so much to tell you."

The phone rang. Max, without looking, said, "It's Aggie. I have to take this."

Maxine didn't say a word as she listened intently to her sister. Her face still held that same serious expression. After a few minutes, she handed me the phone.

"Hello, my precious girl!"

I began to weep, feeling the most human I'd felt in a long time. Hearing her voice reminded me how her love had mattered in the most magnificent way in my life. My parents were young when they had me. Mim had been responsible for me my whole life. I spent five minutes just telling her how much I missed her. She told me stories from my childhood because that's what she did. Anytime I felt uneasy, she reminded me of the best human moments I'd experienced.

"Mim, I'm coming home to the mountain. There is too much going on. I have one thing left to do, and I'll be home in time for one of your famous home-cooked meals tomorrow."

"Emerson, whatever it is, don't do it alone. You are a powerful force, but choose your resources. The Universe is always reaching a hand to us. Emerson Stone, you decorate the parts of my heart that are the most valuable. The thing that always saved you in everything you did was your ability to do what you, and only you, think is best. Your discernment is beyond extraordinary. Emerson, whatever it is, don't forget why I call you Mercy!"

"I'll be home soon, Mim! You should maybe call Edna and see if she can come stay. I don't like the thought of you being alone. I love you!"

"Safe travels, my fierce warrior. Remember my kitchen when you need a boost of comfort. Emerson, you are my greatest joy. I love you!"

I hung up the phone more motivated than ever to get back to my grandmother and my magical mountain. Nyx stared at me in astonishment.

"What?" I asked.

"It's just in all the stories I grew up hearing about the legendary Red Crow of Justice, I have yet to see that in you."

I overlooked her attitude, as she still didn't know what to think of me. I sat them both down, laying out the details of Victor's psychotic tendencies. I made it abundantly clear I wanted to kill him.

After I finished, Ara exclaimed, "It's all coming together, bit by bit! We found the location of another crow sibling by the name of Pearl Rhodes. She's Levi's sister. As a bonus, it was also revealed she was the one initially scheduled to meet your Abel in Budapest with your previous life's femur. As you know, she no-showed, and by the time we found her it was too late. She had mysteriously disappeared, leaving behind a concerned boyfriend who's currently safe with Solomon. It was clear she's been taken.

"What wasn't taken was the bone, along with years of research about Apollo Industries and other organizations of the like. To make an incredibly complicated story short, your would-be father-in-law is trying to control the souls of the world. The alternative spiritual communities have their own sick radicals, and it looks like there's a large population of wealthy aristocrats using magic for their own gain.

"The blood sacrifice feeds human essence to the Divine Beings of the Underworld, who in turn bestow power to the unworthy. Victor's cannibalism was inspired by the cryptic script Hagan and I found in Mexico. It was tied to the legend Apollo Industries has on file about your death. They are using your parts to anchor into an ancient power you have evolved past.

"Having those pieces of your former life scattered around are doing only one thing to you: They're keeping you infinitely, earthly human, destined to never ascend. Also, there is one more thing: Any egregious act done while you're without your evolved crow state will only delay your return home."

"What are you saying, Ara?"

"I'm saying you can't kill Victor."

Nyx spoke up with grand enthusiasm. "Don't worry about it. I'll handle it."

"We'll all handle it." Ara confirmed.

A white crow flew by the window. Esther! I ran outside to see my old friend, who embraced me on sight. The person accompanying her turned around, causing my heart to stop cold.

"Mercy, you look like you've seen a ghost!"

I was frozen. "Who are you?"

"I'm Levi," said the man with the familiar face.

I yelled for Ara and Nyx, "We have to go, now! The woman in the picture, the ear...it's Pearl!"

We left for the Saturnalis' with no plan, me filling in Levi and Esther on the way. Levi's rage was frightening. I was ready to put an end to this nonsense right now. Victor may be only the face of a larger body, but I was ready to cut that face off and send a message to the rest.

There appeared to be no one around except a gardener in the back. Levi entered the home and discovered the picture that had shaken me the night before. His resemblance to the bound girl was uncanny. In a fit of rage, he destroyed the picture and, upon finding no further evidence of Pearl's presence, set the house on fire.

 "Call Abel before he finds out what we're up to and try to find out where his father is," Ara instructed me.

I dialed him quickly.

"There's my Angel of Mercy."

Calmly, I said, "Abel, I have a question about the painting your father showed us last night. Is he at work?"

"Actually, oddly enough, he's headed to your home state to have a meeting with a bourbon distributor. He mumbled something about an 'elixir of life' and left in a hurry several hours ago. You know Father, always chasing money! Mercy? Mercy, are you there?"

My throat was closing as panic filled me. "Yes Abel, I'm here, but something's come up. I'll call you in a few!"

I ended the call without giving him time to answer.

"Auntie Max, call Mim. Victor's on his way to Kentucky. In true fashion, he is not shy about leaving a trail for the world to see. He wants me to come after him."

"She isn't answering." Auntie Max's face was pale.

Esther said, "I'll take Levi and Ara in shift, and we'll get there quickly. Nyx can travel with you via waterway and get you home in half the time it takes to drive."

Auntie Maxine sent a message to LJ, letting her know she was running an errand out of town. "She's my sister. I'm coming, too!"

Ara sent a message while we were en route, saying the kitchen was left mid-meal prep and Aggie was nowhere to be found. I gave her Edna's contact info, holding onto hope that something had come up and maybe Mim had to rush over.

We arrived to find my parents, along with Uncle Ezra and the local police, who were treating Mim's disappearance as a missing person case. Levi and Ara were out scouting for clues. Nyx ran out to find the other crows, while Maxine comforted my mother and Ezra. I told them I would be back and headed to my sanctuary in my cave on top of the mountain.

Uncle Ezra's brand-new truck climbed that old mining road with ease. It ran so quietly. He was right, I did need a new muffler. I cried at the memory of life before all of this. I ran as hard as I could to Saturn's Bridge.

My cries echoed through the caverns. That sick fuck had taken my grandmother, and no matter what anyone said, I was going to kill him.

"You sure about that?" Vetiver swam through the air as Ash popped out from the shadows. "You know I can't let you do that, Goddess."

I melted in his arms at the sound of his voice.

"You have a mission, and I'm here to remind you of it," he said. "The time will come, and you will have your revenge. It just cannot be today. You have much to achieve before you can go creating massive karma for a life that shouldn't matter that much to you."

I slapped him. "This life does matter to me. How dare you?!"

He held me close, subduing me. "Easy, Goddess. I forget how human you are sometimes. I meant no offense."

We sat on Saturn's Bridge looking over the dark water. "I don't want to do this anymore."

"What, life?" He laughed. "I'm afraid that isn't an option, dear. I am intrigued by how quickly humanity has changed you. It's as if you have no anchor controlling the evolution of your emotions. Do not let that get you killed or, even worse, make you do something that will jeopardize your return. Listen, I know you are hurting, but there are changes happening within the entire grand design that need all our attention. Your mission is to heal the human and *then* eliminate the threat."

"Does Esther knows you're here?"

"She doesn't, and she also knows nothing of us. Well, not us now, but us in different concepts of time. The crows shouldn't know who you really are. It's something they'll have to come to slowly as part of their own evolution."

I stood up. "I should probably find the others."

"I've always got eyes on you, Goddess," he said as he disappeared into the darkness.

As I was preparing to leave, I heard a noise. "Ash, is that you?"

"It's been quite the adventure, hasn't it, Justice?" My shadow friend from the veil stepped forward.

 "Men like Victor Saturnali are minor compared to the other evils in this world," he continued. "I know you're mourning your Earth mother's kidnapping. You must remember what happens to the good souls who are trapped by grief. It is a teacher, nothing more. Like you, she chose this path before she ever arrived. Honor the space your heart needs, but don't be blinded by its wounds."

He vanished, and I quickly made my way out to help search for Mim. I decided to drive over to Edna's. I started to worry; what if Mim asked her over for company and they both were taken? Edna's house was only a short drive from the hollow. I pulled in as Edna was emerging from her outdoor cellar.

"Mercy, is that you?"

"Ms. Edna, we've been trying to get a hold of you for hours. Have you seen Mim? She's missing!"

"Missing!" she exclaimed. "Why, I've been working in this yard all day and haven't had my phone with me. Come inside, dear, and I'll make us a tea. You must be absolutely beside yourself."

As we walked into the house, it occurred to me that Ara and Levi had stopped in earlier, and she was not home. "Edna, did you say you've been here all day? We came by earlier, and you weren't here."

"Oh, I must have been in that old root cellar, dear," she yelled from the kitchen.

The sound of tea coming together triggered memories of Mim, until something odd caught my attention. The mask of a golden dragon, just like the one in my vision, was mounted on the wall of the back bedroom down the hallway.

CHAPTER 13

Death of the Mountain

Ms. Edna was the last person I would expect to betray us. I sent a quick message to Ara, instructing her and Levi to come immediately. I scanned the room for clues, hoping to find something that would help me locate Mim.

"Who's that, dear?" Edna returned from the kitchen with two cups of tea.

My heartbeat escalated. I nervously replied, "What?"

"On the phone. Did someone message about my sweet Aggie?"

Suddenly a man walked through the back door. He was wearing a black suit and a cold expression.

Edna grabbed my hand. "Why so nervous, dear? It's just my nephew Charles. He has been helping me fix things around the house. Drink the tea I made for you. It is your grandmother's special blend. It will help calm you down. You know Aggie is always running off to help those in need. She's probably off blessing the mountain as she always does."

There was an undertone in her voice that lacked sincerity, prompting me to get up. I sensed that I was in immediate danger. "I think I'll drive back to Mim's and see if anything's turned up."

Charles rushed me, grabbing my hands, tying them behind my back.

"She trusted you!" I screamed. "Where's my grandmother, you crazy old bitch? What have you done with her?"

"Your grandmother has shared quite a bit about your bloodline myths over the years. It wasn't until you were born that I was certain you were the incarnation we were waiting for. I thought it was your mother at first. But, no, it was not until that cold October full-moon morning, the moment you were born, that I realized it was you. You're the Solomon witch."

Charles carried me out the door and down to the cellar. With a hood covering my head, I descended underground in complete darkness. Surprisingly, I was keenly aware of my surroundings. Fear had not beaten me down because the adrenaline to get to Mim was all I could focus on.

My mind's eye began to open the further we went into the Earth. Just as it presented in the initiation, colors began to flood my inner vision. An opening manifested in my inner eye, allowing me to see a skewed vision of my present surroundings. I sensed an opening ahead filled with people.

Cheers echoed from a gathered crowd. My heart raced as a familiar knowing began to rise. Pearl was in a place like this in my vision. Maybe it was a premonition. I sensed the atmosphere change as we came to an opening in the cavern.

"Ladies and gentlemen, for centuries we've hunted and acquired ancient knowledge to explain the mysteries of human existence."

I didn't need to see the source of that obnoxious, booming voice to identify it. Charles pulled off the hood, and I was horrified to find I was facing about a hundred people. Holding court was none other than the ever-so-arrogant psycho Victor Saturnali.

"I present to you the one and only SOLOMON WITCH!"

The crowd gasped, *then* erupted into cheers.

"This isn't our ordinary annual sacrifice. No, no, ladies and gentlemen, I would not drag you all the way to the middle of fucking nowhere Kentucky for just any old offering. BEHOLD, Emerson Stone, the living reincarnation of the legendary Solomon witch. Legend says King Solomon bewitched a bloodline to make him immortal, giving him the power to control his own soul."

I couldn't help but feel a glimmer of humor deep inside for his misguided information. They were all misguided, so caught up in origins and history when they should be present to an ever-changing timeline. The truth changes the further it travels from the present. The Universe is always teaching us in the now.

"For centuries, the incarnations of Solomon were tracked, only a theory until he brought his witch out into the open. Oh, yes, witch, your jaunts through Europe with Solomon in the 1800s are legendary. The destruction of the Solomon Witch was a plan initiated to trap the old King." He focused on me. "But your King never came, did he?

"As fate would have it, the Turkish chapter of the order discovered an interesting incantation regarding magical enhancement. The more sacred the creature, the more amplification their essence provides to your own conjuring. Add that to ancient scripts or talismans, and you have the world at your fingertips." He laughed manically. "So I decided since the old King failed his witch and we can't seem to find these missing pieces, how about we just cut her body up and create our own booster?"

The room again applauded this lunatic. The ritual table was behind him, and I had to get to Pearl. I needed to see if she was OK. Victor walked close to me, inspecting the ropes that bound my hands.

"How do you feel, Emerson? Is it a bit... aggressive?"

He turned and continued speaking to the crowd. "Her blood will be the offering, and as if that and parts weren't enough, ladies and gentlemen, I present to you Agatha Faye Stone, the grandmother of our little Solomon Witch. The Gods will love us today, my friends!"

I screamed, fighting my way to Aggie.

"Let her go. She can't go anywhere. Let them say their goodbyes. Ritual holders, prepare the space."

"Mim! Oh, Mim!"

Tears streamed down my face as I lay my cheek against hers.

"How did we end up here, Mim?"

I was devastated, in a crazed state, but Mim was ever the picture of wisdom, calm and certain.

"Hush, child, we haven't much time. Pearl escaped. I am here because I created a distraction for her to get free. I knew Edna was up to no good the minute I returned from New Orleans."

Seeing her like this, ready for whatever was to come, only worsened my hysteria. I was a child again in her arms.

"Oh, Mim, what do I do?"

"You do the right thing and live by your name."

"Ara and the crows are on their way. They'll be here any minute. We're going to get out of this, Mim, and when we do, I'll make this right. I will make all of it right."

She looked at me with the same look of peace with which she faced her mountain every morning. Just as I was about to tell her I loved her, the sound of wind came roaring down the cavern. One by one, they flew in with a vengeance: White, Purple, Blue, Yellow, Gray. The cavalry! I looked at Mim to see the joy firsthand in her eyes, only to find Victor holding a knife above her body.

"NO!!"

The knife sank to the hilt into her delicate chest. He turned to make his way toward me. I stood there, numb, unable to run to safety. I never looked away from her for one second until I saw the light leave her eyes.

"Mercy!" Ara's voice pulled me out of my daze as she cut my hands free and made a play for Victor. Out of nowhere, Pearl leaped from the shadows.

"Don't you touch that sick fuck! He's mine!"

"Pearl?" Levi and his sister exchanged glances that instantly relieved and empowered them. They were ready for war.

Victor's guards exerted their force on us, while others began escorting him out. People were running frantically towards a couple of exit pathways. But I had my sights set on one person. Edna was slowly backing her way out of the ritual space.

"Oh, you're not going anywhere, Edna."

I grabbed a knife off a dead guard, Levi's handiwork, and made my way to the traitor. I was surprised at the intensity of the joy in my mind at what would transpire. She would die for what she did to my grandmother.

"Mercy, no! Stop!" Esther pleaded with me. I didn't care. I knew killing someone would destroy the mission, but in this moment that did not seem to matter.

I raised my knife, aiming for her face, when Charles grabbed my arm and threw me to the ground. My head hit the cold Earth, blurring my vision as Vincent stepped from the shadows, Hagan close behind. Vincent grabbed Charles as Hagan grabbed Edna. In one fell swoop, they snapped both their necks, killing them cold.

The kill was so sacred it brought the room to a pause. They'd moved in like mercenaries, bringing death on the back of a hum that could be felt in the air all around. When the sting of death lingers to this degree, it commands its own reverent space. Aggie's body lay lifeless on the stone as my world began to come apart.

We surfaced from the cellar to find the police, our family and half the community present. Hagan emerged carrying my precious Mim's body. Maxine collapsed to the ground at the sight. This woman who had been fierce my whole life was more fragile than I. I had the honor of knowing that grand woman for my short life, but Maxine had ages of memories crippling her in this moment.

Victor, the police were told, was a "family friend" with mental health issues. Law enforcement issued a statewide alert for a murderer at large. There would be no mention of sacrifice, ritual, or any level of truth, for that matter. The world does not want that, and the powers that be want to keep it that way.

Esther, Ara, Hagan, and Maxine returned to Aggie's with me. Nyx returned with Vincent through the cave system, while Pearl and Levi stayed on Victor's trail. The thought of going back to Mim's house without her crushed me.

We arrived at Mim's to find my mom and Ezra finishing the homemade bread she had left unbaked. While the bread was baking, we all sat on the porch in silence. That is what you did on the mountain. It was almost irreverent to speak at this point.

The sky broke open to release a gentle rain, making it seem as if the very stars in the sky wept the loss of such an outstanding being. This day was done, and I had nothing left to give it. Without a word to anyone, I went back to my room, shut the door, and cried myself into a deep sleep.

Morning came too quickly, reminding me all over again that she was gone. Today, we would plan her funeral. My phone finally had a full charge, revealing several messages from Abel. He begged me to call him. With each message, he was more desperate to convince me he truly did not know what was happening. I wasn't choosing this experience for myself right now. I didn't know if I would ever be able to speak to him again.

The smell of breakfast and laughter filled the house. I was happy to have Auntie Max. It was like I still had a piece of Mim. I walked into the kitchen to find Ara, Hagan, and Auntie Max sitting around the table. I ate my breakfast, speaking not one word to them. The second I ate my last bite, Auntie Max asked me to take a walk with her.

Mim's favorite walking trail branched out from behind her house. Maxine, cane in hand, slowly made her way toward the pathway into the woods. Focused on making her way to the clearing, she did not speak. The clearing was a flat, circular space in the middle of the forest. Much like my cave, this was Mim's secret space. Uncle Ezra had built her a beautiful seating area where she could relax and enjoy being among nature.

Maxine held my hand. "Death has this way of shutting us down for a moment. However, the poetic intention of death is to motivate life, not suspend it. Humans often forget they can move with their grief. Sure, there's a time for stillness and reflection, but the quicker you reflect your grieving soul into the mirror of the world, the more you understand its purpose."

"I feel like this was all for nothing," I whispered, tears rolling down my face. "I found out I was part of some bigger cosmic design only to come to Earth to live the fullness of the mission, for what? To feel even more empty? The Universe cruelly showed me the magnificence of my origins, then told me I must earn my way back, and, oh yeah, save the world."

"My, my child, that's a whole lot of self-importance. You think you're some epic hero on your way to your happy ending? There is no happy ending for any of us. There simply is. Happy moments hold their power more efficiently in the present. I may not be a battle crow, but I am a being of magic. I, too, have an awareness of my ascended self. I, too, slip back into the forgetful space of being an average human.

"Emerson, life expands and contracts. Your awareness does the same. Remembering your mission does not have to mean ignoring your grief. You have the power to manage both. Death is just the pause before the return of the next Sun."

I heard a sound close by, as if something were circling us in the woods. A family of deer walked into the clearing, along with several other forest creatures. The air above us filled with what had to be at least one hundred butterflies. The Universe once again reminded us in our time of sadness that we are all connected.

We stood to make our way back down to the house, when I noticed a black fox. Ash kept his distance, but his eyes let me know his sympathy. Maxine was right. My grief was not meant to be a prison.

I returned to the house to find Hagan waiting for us on the back porch. Auntie Max continued into the house. Hagan looked at me with his comforting eyes, and for one moment my grief subsided. That look reminded me that my heart is important, but so are the hearts of the circle.

"Mercy, I'm so sorry about Aggie. I promise we'll make this right."

"'Make this right.' That's an interesting sentiment, isn't it, when we both know nothing's ever absolutely right?"

Hagan gently held my hand, "Don't lose hope, Mercy. She would have wanted you to continue leading this mission to the very end."

"Yeah, losing hope isn't an option," said Pearl as she walked outside to join us.

"Where's Levi? Did you find Victor?"

"Victor managed to escape, but Levi's tracking two of the guards hoping to find a trail back to him. Mercy, I'm here to pay my respects to Aggie. She saved my life."

Pearl was probably the most beautiful human. There was a perfect balance of femininity and masculinity that held such a poetic androgyny it felt divine. I could not help but notice her ear and remember her torture.

She laughed, seeing me looking. "I think it gives me an edge."

"I saw what they did to you in the white room. I had a vision. That's what eventually brought us to you."

Her laughing stopped cold. "You should see what I did to some of them last night."

The words were so intense that neither Hagan nor I needed elaboration. Her tone made it quite clear that she not only killed them but likely handled them in a way that was much worse than anything they gave her. Maxine brought out coffee, and she and Esther and Ara joined us on the porch just as Pearl began to share her story.

"I was snatched off the streets of Budapest, drugged, and shipped to the States. They brought me here, torturing me for days. They wanted the bone I promised them and kept asking for the stone. Victor is searching for what he called a 'heart stone.' The bone was safely tucked away, but I had no idea what stone he sought.

"The white room isn't too far from the space where we all met. The caves in Kentucky are a never-ending system. I heard them holding ritual when some sort of commotion broke out. Then I heard someone chanting an incantation. The underground lighting system went out, and the next thing I knew, Aggie was freeing me.

"Just as the last knot fell to the ground, lanterns began lighting up all around. Aggie ordered me to run as soon as they grabbed her. I didn't leave her. Mercy, you need to know that I did not leave her. I hid in the shadows. As soon as the ritual began, it was brought to a halt with one phone call. Immediately after, you were escorted into the space."

I needed this memory of her last moments. Knowing she walked so boldly into that space and saved a life, I see. I get it. She truly lived her own mission to the end. My grief made me forget who I was for a minute. I would see her soul again, and I would celebrate her like the warrior she was. I hugged Pearl, silently thanking her for the gift of this share.

"That sounds like my fearless sister," Maxine said with gusto. "Her dramatic death will not be in vain, children. Today we take the time to say goodbye to a legend. Tomorrow, we burn the world down until we find them all!"

Hagan's beige suit brought his whole being into a different space. It reminded me of the first time I saw his blue eyes in Mississippi. He was a beautiful man in every way. I was happy to have him by my side to get me through this day.

We arrived at the family tomb on the top of the mountain to find what seemed to be the entire town. I was overwhelmed by the sight of all the love, when all of a sudden a voice whispered in my mind:

Anchor your emotions, Goddess.

Ash and Esther had arrived, looking as if they were in a photoshoot for Italian *Vogue*. They complemented each other perfectly. Ara and Pearl stood close to Maxine, Uncle Ezra, and my parents as the community continued to stream in. I looked around, taking it all in, trying hard not to focus on my personal loss.

"Agatha Faye Stone, woman of the mountain, was born in a cabin not too far from where we stand. Her age, infinite. She leaves in this realm two children, Diana and Ezra, grandchild Emerson Buckley Stone, and myself, along with special niece Louisa May Jones, my daughter. It is Aggie's wish for this ceremony to not linger, for the return to nature moves swiftly when all chapters end. The greatest way to honor nature when touched by the sting of death is to neither get in its way nor run from it. We must move with it and move on."

Sunset opened the door to prepare for its own spiritual ending. We had reached the layer of the descent where the day chooses to surrender to its death. It was appropriate that this grand woman take her final bow in the in-betweens.

Music from Hagan's violin wept into the crevasses of the mountain as they walked her ashes from East to West three times around the tomb. One by one, the crowd began to leave as the ceremony came to a close. The moment the light left the sky, her ashes were placed into the tomb, forever sealing the lifetime that was Agatha Faye Stone.

I started this mission singularly focused on returning to my origins. Humans. We are all conditioned to think we come to Earth to learn to be better, only to return to some origins rooted to a belief system that never stopped evolving. You cannot chase the meaning of a story that never ends. Intellects chasing the sacred meaning of life only further the notion that it can be reduced to a method described from some master manual that holds the secrets of the Universe. In all my incarnations and evolved states, one thing was incredibly clear to me: Everything we need to function in the fullness of our individual missions in this world is inside of us.

You would think we should know this. The fairytales of childhood teach us that we had what we needed all along, but most humans hear that message at the end of the story and forget what it took to access those resources. If not for the grand quest of the fool, we would never know what we're made of. I showed up in this world ignorant to who I was, earning every remembrance of my divinity that came my way. I forgot those highest parts of myself repeatedly. The only return I craved now was the continual return to center.

I had not recovered the missing pieces of my former life. I lost my grandmother. The bad guy got away. Evil still roamed the Earth. But I gained more understanding of my Truth as it stands today in this moment. Knowing your truth holds more power in your evolution than "they all lived happily ever after." The evil in my life will still be there tomorrow.

But so will the divine.

The Quest is far from over.

THE END

East S. M. is an Appalachian Occultist, Diviner, educator, artist, performer, and now author. A cosmic being in her own right, she was born in a small Kentucky town that sits inside a meteorite crater. A wild past of wonderful and sometimes unspeakable experiences, and decades of empowering others to seek their own quests, has called East to share Mercy's story in the esoteric genre of Occult fiction. Her debut novel is the first in an anthology that reimagines the Spirit world, the human condition, and the necessity of both evolution and devolution within our lifetimes.